Lawless Times

Will Pickle was an ordinary man content to live life as a peaceful farmer until the day his wife died and he lost his farm. Bank president Mike Herman thought it a joke to make Will the sheriff and buckle on his guns. But things didn't go as Herman had planned.

There were plenty of men who would like to bring Will down, but his greatest challenge was the mad renegade known as Crazy Charlie. Destined to live in lawless times, Will found the only rule that applied was kill or be killed – and he was more than able to oblige.

C2000004012155

0121   KINGSTANDING
464 5193   LIBRARY

Loans are up to 28 days. Fines are charged if items are
not returned by the due date. Items can be renewed
at the Library, via the internet or by telephone up to
3 times. Items in demand will not be renewed.
Please use a bookmark

Date for return		
2 5 NOV 2006		1 6 MAY 2015
		1 3 NOV 2015
	2 2 SEP 2007	
1 1 DEC 2006		2 0 SEP 2016
3 0 JAN 2007	1 4 OCT 2011	3 0 JAN 2018
1 5 MAR 2007	2 5 NOV 2013	− 8 JUN 2018
	1 0 FEB 2014	
2 9 MAR 2007		2 4 SEP 2022
− 5 JUN 2007		

Check out our online catalogue to see what's in stock,
or to renew or reserve books.

www.birmingham.gov.uk/libcat

www.birmingham.gov.uk/libraries

Birmingham
Libraries

Lawless Times

M. DUGGAN

A Black Horse Western

ROBERT HALE · LONDON

ISBN-10: 0-7090-8164-2
ISBN-13: 978-0-7090-8164-7

Robert Hale Limited
Clerkenwell House
Clerkenwell Green
London EC1R 0HT

Typeset by
Derek Doyle & Associates, Shaw Heath
Printed and bound in Great Britain by
Antony Rowe Limited, Wiltshire

CHAPTER 1

Will Pickle saw them coming. And he knew the purpose of their visit. He recognized the lead rider as Michael Herman, Bank President. Alongside Mike was Simon Parker, big-shot rancher. Will steeled himself. He knew what was on the cards. A few weeks ago the prospect of eviction bothered him greatly. Today he did not give a damn. The two had brought a heavily armed band of men with them. Will sighed; well, if they were hoping for trouble they were destined to be disappointed.

'Howdy there, Will.' Mike Herman was clearly enjoying this moment, for his tone was jovial and there was a grin plastered on his handsome face. The two men had never liked one another, Will not being a believer in deference.

'Howdy there Mike,' Will rejoined, 'Make yourself at home!' He knew the sarcasm was lost on these men.

'Well, there's no easy way about this,' Parker came directly to the point. 'Your loan has not been redeemed. The bank has foreclosed. Fact is, I have bought your spread from the bank.' He coughed awkwardly. 'I'm sorry to hear about your wife and child. Have you buried them on the property? Naturally I will respect the grave-markers.'

'Nope,' Will rejoined, 'they ain't buried here-abouts. Don't concern yourself.' He stood up, a tall, thin man. 'My horse is saddled and my bags are packed. Like I said, make yourselves at home. I'm heading out.'

'Wait!' Mike Herman cried with some urgency and some surprise, because he had clearly not expected matters to take this turn. He'd been looking forward to seeing Pickle beg, maybe even bawl, for everyone knew Will and Gertrude Pickle had been a devoted couple. 'Where will you go?'

Will shrugged. 'I'm damned if I know! Damned if I care. But I am eager to be gone and that is a fact!'

'And without hardly a cent to your name!' Mike Herman observed with a satisfaction he failed to hide.

'So!' Will shrugged dismissively.

'The fact is, Will, there is no need for you to quit town. I've got you a job lined up,' Herman continued eagerly – a little too eagerly, Will thought. Mike Herman was not one to do another man a good turn. Indeed, did he but know it, Herman had come up with the job offer on the spur of the moment. The fact was, Mike Herman had been looking forward to seeing Will Pickle blasted by Simon Parker and his hard-bitten crew.

'So what is this job?' Will asked without curiosity.

'Why, sheriff of this up and coming prosperous

little town. What do you say?'

Will hesitated, Herman was a mite too keen. 'I ain't never seen myself as a lawman,' he rejoined cautiously. 'At heart I'm always going to be a farmer, a man who likes watching his crops grow.' He stopped. The rest of them were looking at him with incomprehension.

'Take the job, man,' Herman urged. 'It will be as easy as eating pie. Earn yourself a stake before you ride out.'

'Will Pickle, you ain't suited to law-keeping.' A grizzled waddy spoke up. 'You take this job and you're gonna get yourself killed. Much as I like you I'm duty-bound to tell you that you ain't up to scratch. Being a lawman ain't as easy as eating pie. It's damn messy and blood gets spilled.'

'Shut up, Moses!' There was a chorus of yells from Parker's men, some of whom, Will noted with annoyance, were grinning. They were enjoying this. He was the butt of their foolish merriment. 'Will can do it. Ain't he a wiz when it comes to hauling iron?'

They were making jest of him. No way could he ride out now. No way could he leave it like this. He squared his shoulders. The no-account varmints had made the decision for him. 'I want a contract, naturally, with a sizeable bonus at the end of the first year. I also need a month's salary in advance. As you have rightly said, Herman, I ain't got hardly a cent to my name.'

'See sense man. Better to be without a cent in your pocket than filled with lead,' Moses cackled.

'Why thank you kindly Moses, but as you can see I

am down on my luck. My wife and daughter are dead. My farm has been repossessed. Mr Herman has made me a mighty fine offer which I am going to accept.'

'On your own head be it. You damn fool,' Moses rejoined, looking as though he had just eaten a sour lemon.

'Well, I'll be heading for town. I might as well familiarize myself with the jailhouse.' Will paused. 'I guess you will be by with the contract. And I'll need to be sworn in.' He grinned. 'Say, I reckon I'll have the power to run undesirables out of town.'

Mike Herman beamed at the man's naïvity. 'You sure will. And no questions asked. I'll see the town backs you all the way.'

'But are you sure about wanting me to run your town?' Will hesitated. 'I feel obliged to tell you I am a man who likes to do things my way. And I ain't a quitter.'

'And that's why I'm giving you the job,' Mike Herman replied jovially, and actually patted Will on the back.

'See you in town then!'

Will headed for the barn. He did not look back as he rode away. He was no fool. That damn spite-filled varmint had given him the job believing that he was gonna get himself blasted sooner or later. It was a joke. A goddamn joke cooked up by Mike Herman. He could read the varmint like a book.

Simon Parker snorted. 'This town is gonna change. The railroad will be coming through one day. Pickle will be plain useless and will very likely get himself blasted, for he is nothing but a two-bit dirt-farmer. I am obliged to you Herman, for selling the land, but I don't reckon you ought to have offered him employment. The man is a loser but I take no pleasure in seeing him killed. Why, any man with eyes in his head will soon peg Pickle for the two-bit lawman he is!'

'You were prepared to use force to get him off his land. You don't give a damn about Pickle!'

'That's different. He would have left me no choice in the matter. But as I anticipated, he went meekly enough and would have done so even without your offer of employment. Now let's ride! We still have the Coopers to deal with. Saul Cooper, being made of sterner stuff than Will Pickles, is likely to pose a problem. So we must keep our eyes peeled. If Cooper looks likely to haul iron he has made himself a fair target. Understood?'

Mike Herman smiled as Will Pickle signed the contract. The tarnished star lay on the desk and now all Mike had to do was swear in the new sheriff. Why, even now over at the barbershop bets were being placed as to how long Pickle would last before getting himself killed. No one expected him to last very long. He was the stop-gap lawman, the two-bit star and the joke of the town.

Having sworn the oath Will pinned on his badge. 'Well, I reckon this town is stuck with me, leastways for the time being,' he observed, knowing Herman had missed the hint of satisfaction in his voice. 'Well, if you will excuse me I'll set about putting things to rights in my town.'

Outside, rain was falling heavily. The streets had turned to mud. At the livery barn just on the boundary of the town Mrs Charlotte Cooper, widow of the late Saul Cooper, had been given temporary shelter by the cantankerous old coot who owned the establishment. Saul Cooper himself was over at the funeral parlour. Simon Parker had generously offered to pay for a simple send-off. Yesterday, so it seemed, Saul Cooper had reached for his shotgun and Bradley Worth, Parker's top gun, had taken off his head.

'There ain't nothing for you to see to,' Mike Herman rejoined. 'At least, not yet awhile!'

Will headed for the door and the rain. 'I must speak to Mrs Cooper.'

'To offer your condolences, no doubt,' Herman observed smugly.

'Hell no! Condolences ain't much use to a destitute widow with youngsters to feed. Why, there ain't one of you varmints concerned as what might become of her. Simon Parker ain't offered her a handout and neither have you. I guess I have just got to set things right.' Whistling cheerfully, Will strode into the rain.

Mike Herman glared after the two-bit loser. Pickle's tone had lacked respect. He guessed the fool was about to offer the widow money. After all, Pickle had just pocketed a month's salary in advance. Well, there would be no more advances. If Pickle handed over his wages the man could root amongst the restaurant trash-cans for all Mike cared. Or beg the leavings from other men's plates. Yessir, and Mike would be sure to spit on his plate before he handed it over.

Will whistled cheerfully as he approached the schoolhouse. This morning Mrs Cooper had expressed her gratitude at his proposal. She had wept tears of joy. There was just one obstacle in the way and Will aimed to remove it. Afternoon had arrived and the rain had stopped, although the street was a quagmire. Every horse that passed down Main Street churned the mud some more. It was a hot, humid afternoon and flies seemed to be everywhere. A few old-timers were already sitting out on the side-walk, watching out for the stage, which was due to arrive later in the day.

'Well, what is it!' Teacher Doggett demanded upon opening the door in response to a persistent hammering.

Will shoved his boot into the door. 'This won't take a moment, Teacher Doggett. There ain't no easy way about it. My late wife told me that you've been beating those young ones real bad. Especially those who ain't got no one to speak up for them. And furthermore, she's heard tell you've been encouraging the bullies to pick on those weaker than them. Fact is, one of your class tried to hang himself on account of you. And then ran off when the attempt failed. That boy may be dead for all we know.' Will paused. 'Now, all this has made me conclude that you are an undesirable and as such I aim to run you out of town.'

'You're mad!'

'Maybe so, but you're packing your bag and shipping out this very afternoon. The stage will be arriving shortly and when it leaves you're gonna be on it.' He tapped his badge. 'Unfortunately for you, Teacher Doggett, I have been appointed sheriff, and as I understand it the sheriff's word is law, 'less, of course, he encounters a faster gun than himself. Now that ain't you, I am sure of it. Fact is I am puzzled as to why one of your old pupils ain't come back and blasted you. Yessir, I am doing you a favour running you out of town. Make no mistake about it! Walking or crawling, you are going.'

Bradley Worth emerged from the saloon and stretched. He felt damn good until he spotted Mrs Charlotte Cooper on the sidewalk along with her children, three girls, and a boy just able to toddle around. The girls carried clothes hurriedly bundled together when Parker had ordered them to leave. Mrs Cooper clung on to the small boy. She ignored Bradley, the man who had blasted her husband before her eyes.

'He brought it upon himself,' Bradley felt compelled to yell. 'For we had right upon our side.' She did not even look at him. And then Bradley spotted Teacher Doggett stumbling on ahead of Sheriff Pickle. The teacher clutched a valise in one hand. His free hand pressed a bloodstained cloth firmly against his ear. Dogget's face wore an expression of fear. It took a moment or so for Bradley to work out what was going on. The sheriff was running Doggett out of town.

'Hold!' Mike Herman appeared on Main Street;

12

clearly he had been summoned. 'What the hell are you doing!'

'Just running an undesirable out of town,' Will replied, quite unperturbed.

'This town needs a schoolteacher!'

'Well, it's got one. Mrs Charlotte Copper is moving into the schoolhouse and taking over.'

'The hell you say. Who do you think you are?'

'Why, I am the sheriff. You got me the job and swore me in.'

'Bradley, get over here and show this lunatic just how much authority he's really got.' Mike Herman hid a grin. This would be worth seeing.

The young gunfighter, a grin on his face, swaggered over. Will found himself wondering whether he was good enough to deal with this hired gun. He waited, knowing he had no choice but to play the cards as they fell.

'Hell!' Bradley declared loudly, 'Do I look the kind of man who is going to concern himself with who teaches the goddamn school. You want this man dead, do it yourself.' With that Bradley swaggered away.

'You listen to me Will Pickle, you no-account bum.' Mike Herman made a fatal mistake. Will's fist connected with Mike's jaw and Mike went down into the mud. He tried to reach for the derringer concealed in his jacket but Will's old worn boot came down with considerable force on Mike's hand. 'You listen to me,' Will yelled. 'A lawman just can't have folk calling him a no-account bum. Why, it makes a mockery of the law. Get on board the goddamn stage, Teacher Doggett. And you, Mike Herman, don't concern yourself with law-keeping matters!' Will slammed the stage door behind Doggett. Uttering a string of profanities the driver cracked his whip and the stage lurched forward.

Doggett's head poked out of the window. 'This man is mad. He's a dangerous lunatic. A threat to you all!' And then the stage was gone.

'I gave you a job and this is how you repay me,' Mike Herman cried, scrambling to his feet as Will's boot was removed. His hand was numb. He could not reach for the derringer without risk to his person from this lunatic whom he himself had sworn in this very day.

'You got me this job because you take a delight in destroying folk. You wanted me to feel happy on account of having a job and a place to stay. That is until some trigger-happy galoot decided to tangle with me. You wanted me to feel fear and terror. Well, it ain't going to happen. My Gertrude is gone. I ain't going to feel afraid at the prospect of joining her sooner rather than later. Fact is, right now I feel like a dead man walking. I ain't got nothing to lose and you had best remember it.' Will thinned his lips. 'But I ain't gonna stand still and allow anyone to blast me. It would not be right. Gertrude set great store in doing what was right and that's what I aim to do whilst I hold this job.'

Painfully aware that he had lost face, Mike Herman walked away without another word. Doggett was right. Pickle was loco. Nor was Pickle as slow-witted as he had assumed. The man sure had hit the nail on the head regarding the motivation behind the offer of employment. Mike had always enjoyed manipulating other folk into situations they could not handle. He got his kicks from watching folk fall apart when things went wrong.

Well, Pickle would not be around for very much longer. Holding on to that comforting thought he stopped to watch two women on the opposite sidewalk. They were on collision course. One of them had to give way. One had to step down into the mud. One of them was Jezabel, the floozie, who owned the saloon, the other was respectable, recently widowed Mrs Charlotte Cooper, who was making her way, children in tow, to the schoolhouse. Jezabel would be expected to step aside to let a decent woman pass but knowing Jezabel, she would not budge. Why, she was quite capable of sending Mrs Charlotte Cooper flying into the quagmire and Will Pickle would be obliged to intervene. The saloon-woman would best him any day.

Both women had stopped, he noted. Some kind of conversation was taking place although voices had not been raised. To his great astonishment Jezabel held out her hand, which was then shaken by Mrs Charlotte Cooper. Both women then stepped down off the sidewalk into the mud, passed by each other and then stepped back on to the sidewalk. Both proceeded upon their way.

Mike Herman lost interest in them both when a commotion erupted in the alleyway adjacent to Jezabel's saloon. There was no sign of Pickle now. Clearly the man had retreated to the jailhouse.

Sheriff Will Pickle made himself a pot of tea, it had not felt right pressing the tip of his blade against Dogget's ear. But it had felt good when his fist had connected with Herman's jaw. He wondered what would have happened had Bradley Worth taken a hand. He guessed he knew. One of them, Worth or himself, would be dead.

As Will sipped his tea, Sheriff Walt Lock was overseeing a hanging. His posse had been tracking the wideloopers for days. These rustlers had made the mistake of stealing steers belonging to Walt's brother Slim. In the fracas two had gotten away but the other seven were done for. Walt planned to hang them high. One at a time! The others could watch until it was their turn to take centre stage. Nor would death be quick and clean, each man would strangle real slow, kicking and struggling at the end of a rope whilst he got his just deserts. And the last man of all would suffer a grimmer fate, for he was destined to be buried neck deep and left to linger. This was Walt's calling card, men hung high and left to rot with the last unfortunate left. Buried; destined to die even more slowly.

As Walt Lock drank freshly brewed coffee and watched his show, Sheriff Will Pickle poured himself a cup of tea. 'Help yourself,' he offered reluctantly, for company had just burst through his jailhouse door, yelling that he was needed.

'But Doc is dead I tell you!' George Green, storekeeper, cried in some consternation, 'Dead in an alleyway adjacent to Jezabel's saloon.'

'Well he ain't going anywhere,' Will observed,

drinking his tea.

'Now look here, Will. I understand you want to grieve for Gertrude but you've taken on the job of sheriff and, well, as a public official you can't sit drinking tea while a man lies dead.'

'But not necessarily murdered! You say there ain't any sign of blood.'

'No!' George agreed.

'Well in that case I aim to finish my tea before I examine the body. Why, George, I would guess that Doc died of natural causes, right there in the saloon, probably occupied with one of the girls at the time, and they have dumped his body out in the alleyway to avoid scandal. Why, the man ate like a hog and drank like a fish, so it's to be expected. Besides which his sister did most of the doctoring, so he ain't gonna be missed!'

'Well it's clear to me, Will, the kind of sheriff you're gonna be. You aim to sit around doing nothing!'

Will shrugged. 'Well that's the way I'd like the cards to fall, George, I won't deny it, but I ain't never been lucky at cards!' He poured himself another cup of tea. 'Rest assured, George, I'm up to the job. I can handle a Colt .45.' He smiled fondly. 'But as Gertrude said, well that ain't something that needs to be broadcast.'

Sheriff Walt Lock drew his Peacemaker and took a pot-shot at the jerking widelooper. He aimed at the man's boot. Being a crack shot he naturally hit his target.

'For mercy's sake man, finish this,' one of the men

waiting to be dispatched cried desperately.

Sheriff Walt Lock gave a feral smile. 'Mercy! Hell I don't know the meaning of the word. You're wrong-doers and that's a fact!'

Over at the undertakers Will, having examined Doc Gatrell's corpse, had come to the conclusion that his assumption was spot on. There were no signs of violence, nor had the man's neck been broken. It only remained to inform Doc's sister Miz Gatrell. Will decided he would tell Miz Gatrell to stay put. Miz Gatrell had been Gertrude's friend. Hell, Will could see no reason why Miz Gatrell should not stay put and carrying on doing her brothers work. Most times recently Doc Gatrell had been plain incapable of wielding a scalpel, a surfeit of whiskey being more inclined to set a hand shaking than to steady it. As Gertrude had often pointed out, it was hard for women to earn a living, and folk hereabouts would rather pay Miz Gatrell to patch them up than do without any kind of doctoring.

Leastways, Will reflected as he set out to inform Doc's sister of that which no doubt she already knew, he'd been spared from having to set foot in the saloon to question the women who worked inside. He knew they would have told him one whole parcel of lies and he doubted whether he would have been able to get any sense out of any of them.

CHAPTER 2

'There's one hell of a ruckus at the schoolhouse,' Old Moses hopped from foot to foot. He was also wheezing. Will guessed the old coot had run all the way to the jailhouse in order to be the first to bring news of the ruckus. He looked up from his wood-carving in some exasperation. 'Fact is,' Moses continued without being prompted, 'Mrs Charlotte Cooper has invited the children from the saloon to attend lessons.'

Will knew that some of the women working over at Jezabel's saloon had kids. By tacit agreement these kids had been kept out of sight until now. They did not attend church nor Sunday school, nor the town's annual picnic.

'And decent folk are protesting,' Moses continued excitedly. 'Miz Jezabel herself is down there, along with that hired gun she employs to keep order in her saloon. It's a stand-off, I tell you. Someone is gonna get blasted.'

Will stood up. He had little interest in the whole damn businesss, but this town was paying him so he little choice but to get over to the school and attempt to calm the volatile situation.

'Ain't you sorry you ran Teacher Doggett out of town?' Moses essayed.

'No I ain't,' Will rejoined as he took up his shotgun. 'There ain't much I don't know about folk in this town,' he muttered. 'And certain folk are not as respectable as they like to make out. There ain't no one in this town fitted to throw the first stone!'

Dogged by Moses he headed for the schoolhouse. The old waddy had taken up residence at the jail, having been sacked by Boss Parker on account of his rheumatism. They heard the ruckus long before the school itself came into view, an angry buzzing punctuated by loud yells.

And, as he had expected, Mike Herman was present, oozing with self-righteous indignation. 'It's about time you showed up, Sheriff!' he observed. 'As you can see, we have need of you. The decent folk of this town are not standing for this outrageous behaviour.'

Voices were raised as men enthusiastically bawled their agreement. Peabody, Miz Jezabel's hired gun, looked uncomfortable, as well he might, for the young gunslinger Bradley Worth was present.

'Do you need a hand, Sheriff?' he enquired smirking with enjoyment. 'Don't be ashamed to acknowledge you ain't in the same league as Peabody!'

'Thank you for your kind offer, Bradley.' Will addressed the gunman. 'But your gun ain't needed. It ain't needed because the good folk of this town are gonna reconsider and once they have thought this matter through they're gonna concede Miz Cooper is right to say learning is for all.'

'Have you taken leave of your senses,' the Reverend Campbell cried, clearly outraged.

'And these folk are gonna reconsider because they know none of them has the right to throw the first stone, not that anyone is gonna be throwing stones. Yessir, they all know they are sinners. Why, we have murderers in this town, adulterers, thieves, liars, the late Mrs Pickle knew them all, womenfolk will gossip amongst themselves and Mrs Pickle had lived in this town a mighty long time. Nineteenth August fifty-four was one of the dates Mrs Pickle mentioned to me. That is when a certain wrongdoing occurred. Yessir, I remember every word my late wife related.' He paused, and there was silence; no one was shouting now. 'And these folk are gonna look into their hearts and see these unfortunate kids are gonna turn into upright citizens on account of attending Miz Cooper's school. Ain't that so, Russell?'

Russell, one of the farmers who but ten minutes previously had been bellowing the loudest, nodded vigorously. 'Yessir, Sheriff Pickle. It sure is. As the Good Book says; let him without sin throw the first stone.'

To the Reverend Campbell's astonishment men and women who had hitherto been proclaiming disgust were strangely silent. He stepped forward, raising his arms as he launched into a tirade, spittle flying from his lips as he spoke.

'Damn right we will, Pastor, damn right,' Steve Clarke yelled as the preacher at last ran out of steam.

'You're a bag of wind, Pickle. Why, I heard tell you never had the stomach to kill your own chickens. Your wife always had to do it. You're a damn yellow-belly coward. Get out of here and leave us real men to do what needs to be done.'

'Well folks, I reckon, having reconsidered, you had best head on back home.' Will ignored the drunken Steve Clarke. There was a sinking feeling in the pit of his stomach. Inflamed by the Reverend Campbell's foolish ranting, Steve Clarke was not going to back off.

'I'm gonna stomp you, Pickle. I'm gonna stomp you good!' Steve Clarke bellowed.

Will backed away slowly raising the shotgun as he did so. 'This ain't your concern. Why, you do not have young 'uns so this really ain't your concern in any event.'

'He's a concerned citizen,' Mike Herman declared.

'Yes, that's what I am. And now you're gonna be on the receiving end of my boot.' Steve Clarke, swinging his huge beefy arms, sledgehammer fists clenched, continued to advance.

With a sinking feeling Will recognized the truth. The fool thought he was incapable of shooting. 'I ain't no rabbit frozen with fear,' Will croaked. 'Back away, Steve. I don't want any trouble. It ain't my way to do harm to other folk!' He prayed that he could avoid the inevitable.

'No, you're a goddamn chicken.' Hunching his shoulders, Steve Clarke propelled himself forward and Will, without having time even to think automatically squeezed the trigger. Clutching his chest, Steve Clarke fell to the ground and lay face staring unseeingly at the sky as blood pooled beneath him. Steve Clarke, known hereabouts as good old Steve, had breathed his last. And it was entirely his own doing.

'Don't you dare say you're sorry you said our kids could attend your school.' Jezabel rounded on a shaking Mrs Charlotte Cooper.

Mrs Cooper collected herself with an effort. 'Most certainly not. I have right on my side. Our town bylaws say all children must attend at least two days a week. I shall draw up a list and you, Sheriff Pickle, must investigate those who fail to attend and rectify their non attendance.'

Will took a deep breath. His stomach was heaving. 'Just leave it to me, ma'am,' he croaked. 'I'll round up those little varmints who are missing their schooling.'

'You! Woman!' The Reverend Campbell pointed at Mrs Charlotte Cooper. 'You are responsible. Have you—'

'That's enough, Reverend Campbell. I am obliged to arrest you. You are a threat to public safety. I'm running you out of town. I just can't have you here, overturning the apple-cart, as they say. Now head towards my jailhouse or I'll be obliged to blast you!'

'You'll see hell-fire because of what you have done today,' the Reverend Campbell yelled.

'Well if that is the case,' Jezabel stepped forward, and addressed Will, 'why don't you visit my saloon. Free liquor and free women. I reckon you've earned it.'

'No, ma'am, I want none of it. I ain't never setting foot in a saloon unless compelled by my civic duty.'

'Why, I am prepared to entertain you myself!' she exclaimed, much put out.

'No, ma'am, I must decline. I very much doubt if I will ever find a woman who could measure up to my late wife's exacting standards!'

'We'll see, Sheriff. We'll see! And the question is, will you measure up?' she was determined upon the last word.

'No, we won't!' Will turned away.

Peabody rubbed his chin. Miz Jezabel would be gunning for Sheriff Pickle – figuratively speaking, that was. He had turned her down in front of the town.

Bradley Worth stared thoughtfully after Will Pickle. The sheriff had raised the shotgun slowly. There had been no fast gunplay. Well, anyone could fire a shotgun at almost point-blank range, Bradley reflected. A Peacemaker was another matter. He doubted Pickle possessed the ability to haul iron with speed. Pickle had been lucky today. And as for what the sheriff had implied, Lord, these folk were mostly farmers and townspeople. Bradley could not believe what Pickle had alleged about 'em, but folk were dispersing, the belligerence and fight drained out of them. Sure as hell Pickle would not be so lucky next time trouble came to town.

Sheriff Walt Lock ignored the talking head that was howling for mercy. He ignored the dangling corpses. He frowned. There was dissent amongst his men.

They were tired. It had been a long ride. 'Those varmints are wounded,' a posse man argued. 'Hell, we've learnt them a lesson they will not forget. Why not call it a day.'

Lock sighed. Patiently he tried to explain, 'Word will get around the varmints got away from me. It'll encourage other wrongdoers to maybe stray into my territory. My rep keeps them out.' He raised his voice. 'Now, we ain't going to vote on this. Men who sign up to ride up with me sign up for the duration and the duration only concludes when I say so! And the fact is I'd feel obliged to blast any man who tried to back out of the deal. Now I know you men have ridden hard and are tired. But I've got to insist you honour your commitment.'

'Well, I reckon the varmints will head for the town of Galbraith,' Jack Jackson, Walt's right hand man observed. 'It makes sense they'll need a doc, fresh horses, food, ammo.' He paused. 'Last I heard the place had a jailhouse but no lawman.'

Walt laughed. 'I don't reckon we'll be needing any jailhouse. Let's ride. With luck we'll get 'em before they reach Galbraith. Any man who starts to flag had best remind himself there are women and whiskey at the end of the ride.'

Upon returning to his jailhouse, once ensured of privacy Will had vomited up his breakfast. Cleaning up, he told himself that there had been no choice. Steve Clarke had always been a mean-hearted varmint and that was a fact. The next stage would be due in a week, so that meant he was stuck with the Reverend

Campbell. That varmint was only gonna get bread and water, for he was the one who had inflamed Steve. He gave a weary sigh. Mrs Charlotte Cooper would be by with her list of truants. And he'd be obliged to hunt them down and see that they attended. And if their folk dug in their heels and refused to send the kids to school, why he'd just have to start throwing his weight around, something he did not care to do. Hell, all he wanted to do was hole up! He was a grieving widower after all!

'Well, Miz Jezabel!' Peabody observed with a smirk, 'word is Will Pickle ain't gonna be around much longer. Mrs Dora Parker has heard what he's gone and done. She ain't having it, ma'am. Looks like—'

'Thank you, Mr Peabody.' Jezabel shut him up with a glance. 'Let's hope what you say ain't the case, for I aim to get better acquainted with Will Pickle.' She turned away. Peabody was looking at her with incomprehension, for she had always told him that she was through with men, who were more trouble than they were worth.

Over at the jailhouse, Will had worked out he was stuck with Moses. The old coot showed no sign of roosting elsewhere. Will had not made mention of the fact that Moses had taken to bedding down in an empty cell and dogging Will each time he went to eat; that way Will paid for both meals. There was no point in stating the obvious. Moses had his pride.

'Have you got anything to say?' Moses asked uneasily.

'Yep. Life is a funny old dog!' Will observed.

'Sure is,' Moses rejoined without comprehension, relieved Will had made no mention of anything else. 'Sure is,' Moses reiterated. 'Why, Miz Jezabel—'

'Now that's enough talk about Miz Jezabel,' Will interrupted hastily.

'Well, I reckon she's taken a shine to you,' Moses persisted. He winked. 'Like you say, life is a funny old dog! Miz Jezabel ain't gonna quit. She's out to get you!'

Will put a coin on the desk. 'Get on over to Ed's Eating-House and get us two pies. Large size. I reckon we've gotta eat.'

Moses took up the coin. 'I heard tell Miz Parker is riled plenty,' he volunteered. 'She don't hold with the way you ran Preacher Campbell out of town and let those saloon kids attend lessons. Boss Parker is gonna listen to her, sure as hell he will, and the only way to shut her up is do something about you.'

'Go get our pies,' Will replied. Before he could say more a loud yell from outside alerted him to the fact that more trouble was brewing.

'Pickle,' the voice held a trace of Ireland, 'you come on out. Your luck has run out. Now it is your turn to leave town.'

'That's Morgan,' Moses volunteered. 'He's one mean bastard and he works for Boss Parker.'

'Well I reckon I've got Miz Parker to thank for this,' Will rejoined.

'She's an upstanding woman,' Moses replied stiffly.

'Who's gonna get men killed,' Will snorted. He slowly stood up. He felt queasy. Moses was watching him with bright birdlike eyes. 'Yep,' Will drawled,

27

'life is a funny old dog. Here I am trying to avoid trouble and it comes looking for me.'

He went out to confront Morgan. With Morgan were two others, nondescript apart from the mean look in their eyes. All three were smirking.

'You've got to leave town,' Morgan stated without preamble. 'You're loco, Mrs Parker says, and that's good enough for me. That good woman is fretting something bad on account of you.'

'I ain't leaving.' Will stood firm. Lord, the bastards weren't taking him seriously.

'Once I finish with you walking out of town will not be an option. You'll be lucky if you can crawl. Alternatively you can be a good boy, beg my pardon for the trouble you've caused, give my boot a lick clean and I'll let you ride on out. I cannot say fairer than that.'

Will spared the boot in question a very quick glance. The goddamn varmint had stood in horse-dung. It was plastered over the toe of the boot!

'You're loco, Morgan, plain loco. and like as not you ain't going to make old bones.' He saw that once again there was no choice. Violence had been forced upon him. Irish Morgan was certainly an intimidating sight, for he was a giant of a man with long, black, greasy hair which he wore in a long plait down the centre of his back. The end of the plait was weighed down with a piece of finger-bone. Will guessed the varmint had hacked that finger off some unfortunate pilgrim whose path he had crossed. Will aimed to keep his fingers.

'Mind you don't wet your pants,' the giant yelled.

'You're looking mighty odd, Sheriff.'

'Give him a booting,' one of his companions encouraged.

'Well, as you know, I ain't never been one to haul iron.' Will hedged. 'Us farmers ain't much when it comes to gunplay.' His gun arm felt numb from fmgertips to elbow whilst the rest of him felt just fine. He realized this must be due to the fact that putting on a fancy display of shooting to impress the late Mrs Pickle was vastly different from the real thing. 'But that ain't to say . . .' he continued, anger beginning to churn at his innards. He didn't much care for Mrs Dora Parker's presumption.

The only person he'd ever taken orders from had been the late Mrs Pickle, a necessity if one wanted to be a happily married man, he'd realized early on. And he liked being sheriff. Wages and food counted. Having time to sit and remember the happy years counted. He was an honest man as well, which was more than could be said for all lawmen. Thanks to his endeavours young ones who would not have set foot in a school were now going to learn to read and write. There was no help for it. He would have to kill Irish Morgan. And maybe the other two! The odds were not in his favour. And as the three had shown themselves to be varmints with no sense of fair play, why, he just had to stoop to their level.

'I'll pay you one month's salary if you let me leave peaceable. Let me get you the money!' He retreated inside his jailhouse, leaving the three standing at ease, all of them grinning and clearly taking him for a fool. But the grins faded as, bringing his shotgun up to the jailhouse window, he blasted away, catching the trio unprepared.

A slug hit Morgan between the eyes. The giant fell even as the other two were reaching. Will blasted them as well for good measure. The smell of gunsmoke hung in the air. Men were appearing on Main Street, for it was as yet early morning and there had been few to witness the event.

'Anyone else want me to ride out?' Will yelled. 'If so now is the time to speak up.'

No one spoke.

'Mrs Dora Parker is responsible for their deaths,' Will yelled. 'So let's hope none of you other females start meddling and if you do let's hope no one listens.'

'He's crazy!' Salvo the Italian barber exclaimed a little too loudly, then he paled as Will rounded upon him. Crossing himself, Salvo retreated inside his barber's shop.

Will felt as though his legs were going to give way. He wanted to vomit. He watched as the dead men were carted away. All around folk were regarding him with condemnation. Could they not see he had not gone looking for this mess. It had come to his door. These varmints were siding with Irish Morgan, a mean hearted varmint who had always taken delight in making others quake in their boots. Why, the Irishman had stomped a man to death on this very street.

'I'll get the whiskey,' Moses cackled.

'No. The late Mrs Pickle did not hold with liquor. There will be none in my jailhouse. Just get us a couple of pies.'

'You cowardly varmint!' a voice bellowed from outside. 'You never gave them a chance.'

'Two-bit lawman!' a second voice yelled.

'Get out of here, you varmints, or I'll blast a few more for good measure,' Will hollered. 'My patience has worn out. I ain't joshing. I reckon I'm the only galoot in this town who does not care if he gets blasted, so I have nothing to lose!'

The door opened cautiously and Moses came in with the pies. 'Boss Parker won't be pleased.'

'Ah, to hell with Boss Parker,' Will rejoined. 'Killing gets easier, ain't that a fact? And it's being forced upon me. I just can't avoid it and that is another fact!'

Betty Gatrell squared up to Manning the undertaker as he emptied the pockets of the dead. When he refused to hand over half the proceeds she threatened to haul the sheriff over. Manning paid up. 'I have to live,' she yelled. 'And it looks like Will is going to kill more than he is going to wound. But even so, if I am to do the doctoring work I needs must employ a girl to attend to matters such as laundry and baking.' She sniffed, her incompetent brother had certainly sent employment Manning's way.

CHAPTER 3

'You ain't fast enough. In a fair fight you would be done for!' There was a note of censure in Moses's voice that Will did not much care for.

'Staying alive, Moses,' he rebuked. 'That's what it's all about. Staying alive and keeping my job.' He did not point out that were Irish Morgan sitting behind the sheriff's desk Moses would have been given his marching orders. Mechanically he chewed his pie, thinking that he was more than fast enough when it came to hauling iron, his problem was that he was unaccustomed to this sort of thing. He'd always been a peaceable man. Violence was not his forte.

Moses had proved to be a garrulous old coot and talked enough for the both of them. 'Well, I reckon Mike Herman has headed out to tell Boss Parker what you've done,' Moses continued.

'I reckon,' Will agreed.

'You ain't got it in you to be a fast gun,' Moses persisted. 'It takes years of practise!'

'You reckon?' Will muttered.

'Your standing in this town is zilch. They're always gonna think of you as a no-account coward!'

'You reckon?' For all Will cared the old coot could ramble all day.

'Ain't you never going to get round to whittling anything but ducks?' Moses gave up.

Will smiled drily. 'I aim to progress to horses. There ain't nothing like whittling to calm the mind.' The latter statement, he saw, was quite lost on the old waddy.

Simon Parker controlled his rage with difficulty. He could scarcely believe what Herman had related. 'So why did you offer Pickle the job of sheriff?' he asked quietly.

Mike Herman shifted uncomfortably. 'To be truthful, it was my idea of a joke. Whoever heard of a dumb-witted farmer handling the job of lawman? I just wanted to see Pickle flounder around awhile making a fool of himself.' Herman paused. 'But the man is clearly crazy. And he is a coward also. Yessir, he is a vicious sneaky little rat.'

'Well, for a dumb-witted farmer he ain't done too badly. He's enraged my good lady. She thought highly of Doggett and the Reverend Campbell. And he has shown he does not balk at killing. What else do you think he might be liable to do? Can you tell me that! No, I don't reckon you can because Pickle is a loose cannon. He's proved himself obstinate. He's proved himself dangerous and he is tricky. Now you listen good! I want him gone. You pay him off. You offer him a year's salary in advance. All he's got to do is ride on out of town.'

Mike Herman started to protest.

In an instant Simon Parker had sprung up from his desk and grabbed Mike Herman by the coat. His eyes bulged and his face reddened with fury. 'I ain't asking,' he bellowed, 'I'm telling you. This is your mess. Clear it up. Pickle is mad and sly and dangerous. You offer our grieving widower sympathy and cash. I want him gone. My wife is going to give me hell whilst he is around. Irish Morgan deserved better than to be shot down without warning.'

'Why not send Bradley Worth?' Herman grunted as Parker released his coat.

'Because we ain't too far from territory controlled by Walt Lock!'

'So?'

'Irish Morgan acted without my say-so, if anyone asks. But Worth is another matter. He is my trouble shooter and everyone knows it. Lock's another crazy. If he got wind that a rancher had sent his top gun after a lawman why, good old Walt Lock is crazy enough to come on over to investigate. We don't want his kind in our town. You see Mike, when you deal with crazies it ain't possible to know what they're gonna do. Lock has got this bee in his bonnet about upholding the law and putting the fear of the Lord into the wrongdoers. I've heard tell he takes a couple of heads from time to time and sticks them up just outside his town with a message warning troublemakers to keep on riding. Now we ain't wrongdoers but killing a lawman might send out the wrong kind of message. Now you offer Pickle the money and get him of town.' Parker's fist hit the desk with an almighty thump, 'I'm not asking. I'm goddamn telling you. I've got a bad feeling about Pickle, a real bad feeling. Now get on out of here before I boot you out! You are useful to me, Herman, but this time you have gone a step too far. Your goddamn joke has backfired!'

Over at the Painted Lady saloon Jezabel leaned against the bar. 'I like a challenge,' she declared as she downed a glass of whiskey. Peabody, by virtue of being her employee, was forced to listen. Nor was he offered a drink, for he was on duty, as she called it. 'And Will Pickle is proving himself a challenge,' she continued.

Peabody seized his chance. 'Why, Miz Jezabel, it sure is a shame you ain't never learned to bake,' he declared.

'What the hell are you talking about, Peabody?' She poured herself another glass.

'Why, ma'am, I've just seen Mrs Charlotte Cooper heading for the jailhouse with a basket over her arm and unless I am mistaken there is a mighty fine cake in that basket.' Peabody had difficulty keeping a straight face. 'She's making a play for him, I reckon!'

'We will see about that. It is time I thanked him for his intervention at the schoolhouse.' To Peabody's astonishment she whacked the batwings open with considerable force as she went out. He picked up the full glass of whiskey she had left and downed it with satisfaction.

'Well, Sheriff, aren't you going to offer me a cup of tea?' Mrs Charlotte Cooper sat down. 'I'll pour while you cut the cake.'

'I reckon.' Will was not sure what to make of this, not that he had much chance as the door of his jail-house was opened with considerable force, which had him reaching for his .45 before he realized that his caller was none other than Miz Jezabel. The two ladies, he saw, were glaring at each other.

'Will Pickle,' Miz Jezabel cried, 'never mind that cake. I'm giving you a thank-you that ain't going to be forgotten.' Before Mrs Cooper's scandalized gaze she grabbed Will, practically hauling him over the desk, and planted a kiss firmly on his mouth.

'Have you no shame, Jezabel?' Mrs Cooper cried. 'Sheriff Pickle is a respectable man.'

'Honey, there ain't no such thing as a respectable man and I should know!' Miz Jezabel declared shamelessly.

'What the hell is going on in here?' David Russell came through the door. 'Don't bother to explain. Pickle, you've got matters to attend to. I reckon this town is going to have itself a hanging. Muriel Benson has just murdered her man. Fact is, she has battered Nate's head to a pulp with a hammer.' He paused. 'You women get on out of here.'

'We ain't moving,' Miz Jezabel declared. 'Ain't that right, Mrs Cooper?'

'Indeed. We are staying here.'

'Are you going to stand for that, Pickle?' Russell demanded.

'Well I know better than to start man-handling females,' Will Pickle muttered uncomfortably. 'Anyway where is Mrs Benson?'

'Why, me and the boys have got her tied up in my wagon.'

Will rubbed his chin. 'Well, I reckon you had best send for Miss Gatrell.'

'She ain't needed. Nate Benson is dead.'

'Well, I mean Mrs Benson might be in need of medical treatment. Go send for Miss Gatrell anyway. And bring Mrs Benson into the jailhouse. Nate's been taken to the undertaker, I presume.'

'Yep. We brought him in the wagon along with Mrs Benson.'

Mike Herman heard all about it when he got back to town. David Russell waylaid him especially to tell him all about Will Pickle. One or two other concerned citizens also expressed their disquiet.

'He ain't even keeping her at the jailhouse,' Sutton the blacksmith declared in disgust. 'Miz Jezabel is keeping her under lock and key over at the saloon. It seems those three women decided it wasn't seemly for Pickle to have charge of her. He ain't got no backbone. He just went along with them, saying that either Mrs Charlotte Cooper or Miss Gatrell must check on Mrs Benson every day and report back to the office as to her condition.'

'You don't mean to say Mrs Charlotte Cooper and Miss Gatrell have agreed to set foot in a saloon!' Mike Herman was astonished.

'Yes I do. In pursuance of doing their duty, as they call it, they have agreed to do it,' Sutton declared. 'On account of Will Pickle solemnly promising his late wife that he would never set foot in a saloon.'

Mike Herman headed for the jailhouse. Parker was right. Pickle was crazy and totally unpredictable. He found the sheriff behind his desk, whittling away. Another damn duck by the look of it!

Mike forced a smile on his face. 'It must be mighty

hard for you, Will, staying on in Galbraith, being constantly reminded of your loss. How long were you and Mrs Pickle wed?'

'Twenty years.' Pickle carried on with his whittling.

'You need to see pastures new. You need . . . well, I don't know what you need. But I do know you don't need to stay around Galbraith. I'm prepared to offer you one year's full salary, right now. You can go to wherever you want to go. Maybe see New York City. What do you say?'

'Yep. But what about Mrs Benson?'

'Why, the circuit judge has been sent for. She'll be tried fair and square and hung. Leastways you won't have to officiate at the hanging. You'll be spared seeing a woman dangle.'

'I seen a hanging once,' Pickles mused as he whittled away. 'I was a boy at the time and the memory has stayed with me all this time. It ain't a pretty sight, for they do not die quick. The neck ain't snapped as one might suppose. They slowly choke to death, kicking away. Indeed my pa was so disgusted with the spectacle he pulled down hard on the hanging man's feet in order to facilitate death and passage into the hereafter.'

'Well, as I say, you'll be spared having to witness Mrs Benson meet her maker.'

'Well, I can't say I ain't tempted. But if I quit now I'd be fleeing adversity, failing in my duty. Nope, I've gotta see this matter through. I cannot see yet how this matter is going to conclude but I can't leave yetawhile. Besides which, if I left the town council would surely boot Mrs Cooper out of the school-house and Mrs Benson, whose mind ain't quite right at the moment, would be locked up in the jailhouse under the eye of a galoot who would not possess the same exacting standards as myself.'

'Take a look at the money!' Herman placed a wad of bills on the desk. 'And now tell me about your exacting standards.'

'I already have,' Will rejoined. 'You'd best take back your money, Herman.'

'A lawman needs to be a fast gun and that's a fact. You ain't, Pickle. Yep, you can do just fine when you shoot from cover, catching good men unaware, but you ain't up to scratch, you're a loser and you know it. Can't you see I'm doing you a favour?'

'Like you did when you offered me the job,' Will declared. 'Get on out of my office, Mike. Go and report back to Parker. Just tell him I want a peaceful life, for I am a peaceable man, killing is against my natural inclination. He knows Irish Morgan brought death to himself. Any man who threatens a lawman, especially in front of a town, well, that man ain't thinking straight. We all know Irish Morgan did his thinking with his fists and boots, don't we? Now get out of here.' He guessed Herman would make haste to report back to Parker. Sure as hell, with his hired guns Parker was top dog around here. Leastways he had been until now!

Simon Parker came into the jailhouse with a smirking Bradley Worth at his heel.

'Morning, Boss Parker.' Moses was kind of hoping Boss Parker was here to give him his job back.

Parker glanced at the old waddy. He was a businessman, a successful rancher; charity did not figure in his thinking. He'd noticed Moses had gotten mighty slow and had dispensed with the old man. 'Just wait outside, Moses. I want a private word with the sheriff.'

'Sure thing, Boss Parker.' Moses shuffled out. He had spent a lifetime obeying orders.

And me, Will thought, *me, I've never cottoned to taking orders. I'm my own man and glad of it.*

'Let's get one thing straight, Pickle,' Parker began without preamble. 'This is my town. I've watched it grow. I watched people come and go, die and thrive. We do things right in my town. I'll overlook the fact that you've run two good men out of town, that you've put a fool woman in charge of the school and that you ain't got a certain Mrs Muriel Benson locked up in your goddamn cell. Why is that?'

'She's safely under lock and key at the Naked Lady saloon,' Will rejoined mildly. 'As Miss Gatrell will tell you, Mrs Benson is somewhat crazed, she's taken to screaming and kicking and tearing off her clothes. Well, it ain't fitting having a woman like that at the jailhouse, no sir, I can't have a near-naked woman in my jailhouse. I'm a respectable man,' he concluded mildly enough. 'You go on over to the Naked Lady. You can listen to her screaming and kicking and hammering on the door. That kind of business does not trouble Miz Jezabel.'

'Very well, Pickle, I accept your explanation. But,' Parker's fist hit the desk with a resounding thud, 'lunatic or not, that woman is going to hang. She smashed her husband's head to pulp with a hammer. I've seen his body.'

'Well, a jury must find her guilty and a judge must sentence her. If we're doing things right in your town we cannot have a lynching, can we, Mr Parker?'

'I'm not suggesting we lynch her. I'm saying she's gonna be found guilty and sentenced to be hung. And it's gonna be done forthwith. She deserves it. She's done wrong. She's got to be punished and there it is. You've sent for the circuit judge?'

'Hickson, the hanging judge?' Pickle rejoined.

'The very same,' Parker nodded approvingly. 'Now, Will, if you listen to me maybe we can work together.'

'Then why did you send Irish Morgan after me.'

'I'm afraid Mrs Parker was responsible for that little fracas.' Parker managed to smile. 'That's women for you.'

'Yep, they are contrary creatures,' Will rejoined drily.

Bradley Worth, who had kept alive by virtue of his fast gun and his wits, had realized that Pickle had not answered the question regarding whether he had sent for Hickson. Worth kept silent. Boss Parker had never required his employees take an interest. He gave the orders and that was that.

'Well, I will be in town to see justice done. And I have put the erection of a scaffold in hand. I'm going over to the Naked Lady.'

'As you wish,' Pickle grunted without much interest as he returned to his whittling. The Naked Lady smelt of cigars and cheap whiskey, smells he could not abide.

'I demand to see Mrs Benson,' Parker glared at Miz Jezabel, as if daring her to defy him.

'Follow me. This way, gents.' She sauntered upstairs, wide hips swaying. Bradley Worth found himself wondering . . . and Miz Jezabel, glancing over her shoulder, caught his expression and clearly guessed the way his thoughts were going. 'When a galoot's ears start turning red I reckon I know what's going on in his head,' she observed quite coldly. 'Put those thoughts out of your head. I own this place. I leave the entertaining to others. Now here we are. Muriel Benson, you have a visitor. Big-shot rancher Simon Parker, here to see you ain't skipped town.'

From behind the locked door came a high-pitched scream and the sound of fists beating against the wood.

'Now, as she is a respectable woman and as she ain't decent it ain't decent for you to go barging in. Just take a look through the keyhole.'

Stooping, Simon Parker peered through the keyhole. 'Yes, I see what Pickle was talking about,' he declared, reluctant to look away. 'Just be sure that when she has to appear before the judge she is respectably clothed. Get Pickle to handcuff her hands behind her back, that will stop her ripping her garments. And a gag will stop the screeching. With Pickle in charge I can see I have to think of all possibilities. Her trial ain't going to be a farce. It will be conducted proper. Understood?'

'I sure do, Boss Parker. I sure do.' And before he realized her intention she had pinched a stooping Bradley Worth hard upon the ear. 'An undressed respectable woman ain't a sight for you, young man. Ain't that so, Boss Parker?'

Parker grunted his assent. Bradley Worth was grinning. 'You can pinch my ear any day, Miz Jezabel, and anything else you might care . . . And as you ain't exactly—'

'Now that is enough of that kind of talk, Bradley Worth. You'd be foolish to rile me, more foolish than you realize. And now let me treat you both to a drink on the house,' she offered.

'Just one.' Simon Parker downed his beer. It was as he had thought; no one in Galbraith seemed concerned about the impending fate of Mrs Muriel Benson. 'If Will Pickle cannot perform this particular duty, I must officiate myself,' he ruminated, 'Care must be taken to tie the skirt around the ankles. We want no unseemly display. It might be as well to order the womenfolk from the street when the event takes place.'

'Well, some might say a hanging itself was mighty unseemly,' Miz Jezabel observed.

'Nonsense, woman. Wrongdoers must be punished. Others must be deterred. Justice must be done.'

'And to hell with Mrs Muriel Benson!' Jezabel raised her glass.

'You ain't sent for the circuit judge!' Moses essayed.

Will shrugged. 'I'll get around to it by and by.'

'You aim to cross him,' Moses observed. 'Boss Parker ain't a bad man, but he comes down hard on those who cross him. That woman is going to hang,' Moses continued. 'There ain't nothing you can do about it.'

Will suddenly grinned. 'A man can achieve his purpose by doing nothing at all, Moses. Remember that.'

CHAPTER 4

The gunman rode into the town of Galbraith, fury in his heart. Varmints, he observed, were already at work erecting the scaffold. They whistled cheerfully as they worked, exchanging quips with each other. A townsman cursed as he hit his finger with a hammer. Children played roll the hoop. Bonneted women watched.

'Si,' Salvo the barber, who had been watching the construction, replied eagerly. He loved to talk. 'A woman who has murdered her husband; beat him to death with a hammer whilst he was sleeping. A terrible thing, a terrible thing.'

'Where is she? At the jailhouse?'

'Nope!' a bow-legged wady exclaimed. He aimed a mouthful of chewed baccy at the dirt. 'Nope!' he reiterated. 'Fact is Pickle, our lawman, well he just ain't up to scratch. Fact is Mrs Benson is locked up in Miz Jezabel's private parlour over at the Naked Lady saloon. Miz Gatrell and Mrs Charlotte Cooper, respectable womenfolk, look in on her every day. There's one of them now. Mrs Cooper the school-teacher.'

The gunman eyed the black-clad widow who was now entering the Naked Lady saloon.

'What's a respectable woman doing going into a saloon?'

'Well, like I told you, Pickle ain't up to scratch and he is crazy as well. Seems he promised his late wife never to set foot in a saloon. When she has checked on Mrs Benson, Mrs Charlotte Cooper will report to Pickle. That's how it works.' The waddy grimaced. 'Say, stranger are you staying around for the hanging?'

'When is it?'

'Just as soon as the judge gets here. Seems he has been delayed.'

Moses snored, real bad. Will ignored the snoring. The old-timer was passed out in one of the cells. Will stood up. He stretched and reluctantly set out to patrol the town. It was part of a lawman's duty, he had been told, the night patrol to check all was well. He kept his eyes peeled, for he knew darn well that there were plenty in this town who did not wish him well.

A woman staggered along the sidewalk. Will stopped abruptly. Light spilled out from the batwings of the Naked Lady but the sidewalks were deserted now. Men were inside drinking and respectable womenfolk were at home.

'Get on home,' he ordered. 'It ain't safe to be wandering the sidewalk wearing a nightgown.' He guessed she was from one of the shacks on the outskirts of town, a few women plied their trade from the shacks, drunkards who could not get work in Miz Jezabel's saloon.

'Will Pickle, you are a card!' she slurred, throwing herself into his arms.

It was then that he felt hard steel pressed against his back. He had been outmanoeuvred. Someone had got the drop on him. With a laugh the woman hurried away. She had been paid to waylay him, he realized.

'One wrong move and I'll blast you in half,' the voice warned. He did not recognize the speaker. 'I'm gonna tell you what you're gonna do. Understand?' The muzzle of the Colt .45 was jammed harder against his back.

'I reckon,' he rejoined. He had a hunch that if he made a wrong move he would indeed be blasted in half.

'We're gonna mosey over to the Naked Lady. You and me! And we're gonna go upstairs and check on Mrs Muriel Benson. You're gonna tell Miz Jezabel you want the goddamn key.'

'I reckon,' Will agreed.

'You're gonna smile and look agreeable. Now I'm gonna holster my gun before we go through the batwings. I'll be behind you. One wrong move and you are a dead man. Savvy?'

'Sure thing.'

Will entered the Naked Lady saloon. This time he did not have a choice.

'Come for a drink, sheriff?' a voice yelled.

'No. He's come to sample Miz Jezabel's hospitality,' another quipped.

46

'Just doing my duty,' Will replied.

'Why, Sheriff Pickle!' Miz Jezabel greeted him with a smile.

'I'm duty bound to check on Mrs Muriel Benson,' Will replied. 'And if I may say so, I'm mighty glad to see you, Miz Jezebel. If you'll just give me the key to your private parlour I'll mosey on up.'

'With pleasure, darling!' She knew at once something was wrong. 'Best knock loud and hard, let Mrs Benson know you are coming in,' she advised. 'Yes,' she continued, 'I know women and you must knock and let her know lest you scare the poor creature.'

'Yes ma'am.' He guessed he must take her advice although he wished he knew right now what was going on in Miz Jazabel's head.

He climbed the stairs with the young killer close on his heels. He kept quiet, knowing the man was in no mood to parley. 'Well,' he said halting before the end door, 'We must do as Miz Jezabel advises.' He accordingly knocked loudly and called out, all the while conscious of the cold steel pressing against his spine. He then opened the door and walked into Miz Jezabel's parlour. It sure was dim for the heavy brocade curtains had been drawn.

'Ma,' Gabe said but that was as far as he got as he was struck across the arm with a poker. He went down, helplessly dropping his Colt .45, and ended up on the floor with Pickle's boot pressed firmly against his wrist which by now was awash with pain.

'Lucky for him Miz Katy ain't knifed him,' a voice he recognized as Miz Jezabel's observed as she stepped into the room kicking the door shut behind her. At the same time a lamp was lit and light flooded the room. 'Let the varmint up,' Miz Jezabel ordered for by this time she had his weapon.

Gabe lurched to his feet. The girl who had brought the poker down across his wrist was smiling unpleasantly as she settled down in a chair, revealing a great deal of black stocking. Giving him a wink, to his great shock she lit herself a cigar.

'Now then, Miz Katy, I am a respectable man.' Will Pickle uttered the rebuke to Gabe's disbelief.

Katy pulled her skirt down with a grin. 'I might have known that would be all the thanks I'd get from you, Will Pickle. Miz Jezabel and me, why, we have saved your hide.'

'Now then, Katy, Will Pickle ain't interested in your legs,' Miz Jezabel rebuked. 'There is only a certain pair of legs that interests him and that's a fact!'

'I ain't interested in anyone's legs, Miz Jezabel,' Will felt obliged to say.

'Now that's a damn lie, Will Pickle. I saw you looking when the wind blew up my skirts.'

'No, Miz Jezabel, you never did,' Pickle protested.

'Where the hell is my ma,' Gabe cried in disbelief. 'I've come here especially to save her and she ain't here.'

'Well, I could have told you that if you had enquired,' Pickle rejoined.

'Where the hell is she?'

'On the way to England by now,' Miz Jezabel replied. 'Peabody, my man, has escorted your ma and one of my best girls to the coast. They are heading for England, a distressed gentlewoman and her daughter. You see, one of my girls upped and married an English lord. She'll take them in. Distressed gentlewomen go down well, so she tells me. Folk will be falling over themselves to help out. And Miz Susan will do her damnedest to find herself a rich husband. Your ma will have a new daughter and rich son-in-law pretty soon, I reckon!'

'Yep, it seemed the best way out of this mess,' Will Pickle observed. 'It appears your ma was provoked by your late pa. I just could not stand by and let her hang. This way she is gone and out of harm's way and I have avoided unnecessary confrontation with the citizens of this town. I ain't even sent for the circuit judge yet. And when he does arrive, when it is time to escort your ma to the courthouse, why, I will discover that one of the ladies had forgotten to secure the door. It being well known that women can be forgetful,' he concluded before adding with satisfaction, 'The problem has been solved and no one has been killed A good result, would say.'

'If you ladies have no objection I intend to get out to the doc's place. My wrist, my gunhand,' Gabe snarled, 'is in need of attention.' Oddly enough he did not think that Pickle would endeavour to run him out of town, because Pickle himself was nodding and saying he must get back to his office.

'Can I tempt you, Will?' Miz Jezabel cried.

'No, Miz Jezabel, you cannot.' Pickle backed hurriedly out of the parlour.

'You cause trouble for Will Pickle and you are done for,' Miz Jezabel hissed at Gabe.

'I throw a mighty mean blade,' Miz Katy added. Gabe, who once would have laughed at these words, kept silent. The set-up in this town was mighty odd. Pickle was the damnedest sheriff he had ever encountered, but Pickle sure as hell was mistaken if he believed he had avoided confrontation over this matter. The men of this town would not see it that way, nor swallow Pickle's flimsy excuse.

'I'll do it for you!' Mike Herman offered with a leer. He had spoken loudly and men pricked up their ears, 'Clearly you ain't up to putting a noose around a woman's neck, a necessary part of law keeping,' Herman continued. He had accosted Pickle as he was walking past the now finished scaffold.

'No need for that. I shall carry out my law-keeping duties,' Pickle rejoined.

'Any other lawman would have run that young killer out of town,' Herman lowered his voice but the words still carried. 'Any man who wears his Colt .45 slung low is a gun for hire. And you ain't said a word to him. You're running scared and that's a fact.'

'Well, as no one in this town is hiring I ain't got nothing to worry about,' Pickle rejoined. 'That's how I see it, in any event. He'll up and ride out when the mood takes him. I avoid confrontation whenever I can. And I would advise you and Parker to follow suit.'

'You ain't fast enough to take him on!' Herman made it sound an accusation.

'Well, I don't aim to find out,' Pickle replied.

'Yep. We all knew the late Mrs Pickle wore the

pants—' That was as far as he got for Will Pickle, with a snarl of rage, punched him full on the mouth. As Herman went down Will booted him.

'We'll have no disrespectful talk about the late Mrs Pickle,' he hollered, clearly enraged. 'You've gone a step too far, Mike Herman. I sure as hell would feel obliged to blast any varmint who disrespected the late Mrs Pickle.'

Mike Herman, using the gallows as a prop, hauled himself to his feet. He wiped the sleeve of his smart new grey jacket across his mouth. The sleeve came away stained with blood. The new gun in town, the man called Gabe, had appeared and was watching with a sneer.

'If you do not object, Sheriff Pickle,' Herman managed to keep a steady voice, 'I intend to call in at the telegraph office. The circuit judge has been delayed far too long.'

Will Pickle shrugged. 'Please yourself.' He did not turn away; Mike Herman looked mad enough to try and back-shoot him.

'You have not even sent for him!' Herman accused as realization dawned.

'I have had other matters on my mind.' Pickle did not bother to deny the accusation.

'Yes,' a waddy yelled out. 'Like avoiding Miz Jezabel. I'm betting on Miz Jezabel. No offence intended.' Good-natured laughter followed this joshing. And even Will Pickle managed to smile.

'Well then, you're gonna lose,' he rejoined mildly.

Mike Herman strode away painfully aware that he was no longer the centre of attention here. Nor did

Will Pickle hit a man of his standing and get away with it, as the sheriff would learn to his cost.

Gabe Benson wanted to kill Mike Herman right now, but if he were to do that he would find himself facing the sheriff, and Pickle, after all, had saved his ma. Most lawmen would have decided why, hell, the town did not even need a circuit judge as the woman was clearly guilty of murder, but not this unusual man who had prevaricated and sent Gabe's ma on her way to safety.

'Look her up six months from now,' Will had advised. 'But do it discreetly. Don't draw attention to yourself. Try and pretend you are a gent! No one will know you ain't nor that killing folk is your forte.'

'What do you mean, folk? I ain't never gunned down a woman or a young one!' Gabe had rejoined indignantly.

'No slur intended.' The sheriff had immediately apologized.

Controlling his urge to kill Mike Herman, Gabe followed the man to the telegraph office. He loitered outside, enjoying Herman's bellow of rage when it was confirmed that no request for the circuit judge had ever been made. 'Get him here pronto,' Herman commanded the telegraph clerk importantly. 'Get him here pronto, this town is going to have itself a hanging.'

'Yessir,' the telegraph clerk agreed. 'Bill Fowles from the restaurant was asking whether it would be in bad taste to set up a pie-table near the scaffold. He could earn a mite extra, he said.'

'I do not see why not,' Mike Herman pompously

agreed. 'Why, am sure I can think of no one on the town council who might object.'

'Well you see, Fowles kind of thought Pickle might turn loco again and smash up his pie table,' the telegraph clerk continued.

'I think not. We will have a guard put on that table just in case our two-bit lawman takes a turn for the worse. Anyway, you tell Fowles not to worry about the sheriff. The man is a lunatic without a doubt. Hell, if we could just get him shipped to an asylum and find ourselves a decent lawman we'd know where we are!'

'Yessir.' The clerk nodded. 'Why, we have a reply already. The judge will be with us as soon as he possibly can.'

'Excellent. I will inform Pickle myself.'

As it was, as Gabe observed, Mike Herman was compelled to yell the news through the door of the jailhouse, since Will Pickle flatly refused to open up, yelling back that he did not give a damn about the circuit judge!

'So what are you gonna do when Simon Parker brings his men into town and orders you out?' Moses asked with interest.

'Do you know something I don't?'

'So what are you gonna do if they wind you in chains and decide to ship you to an asylum?' Moses continued. 'Yessir, you may smirk, but I ain't always been an old coot working for big-shot Parker. I was a young man once. I travelled the land and I seen it all. I've seen a mob storming the jailhouse, I've seen a no-account sheriff being ordered out of town, I've seen a man, not a lawman, mind you, being chained like a dog and shipped East to an asylum. I've seen it all and you ain't, for you have passed your life as a two-bit farmer. So what have you gotta say?'

'I'm riding out to Gertrude's grave. I'm gonna sit and ponder a while on what you have said. But I don't see myself as a no-account sheriff.'

'Well, no offence intended, but sure as hell that is how others in this town see you and it makes one hell of a difference.' Moses winked. 'A few ladies excepted, but they don't count.'

'Like I said, I am riding out and I intend to sit and ponder upon what you have said.'

'Hell!' Moses exclaimed, 'I wasn't wanting you to sit and ponder. I was telling you to get out of this two-bit town while you still can. This town belongs to Parker and Herman and sure as hell they ain't no friends of yours!'

The town of Colgan was not much of a town. But even upon being given confirmation that two men, one young, one old, both wounded, had passed through Sheriff Walt Lock decided to linger. His men needed a break. They would stay until mid-morning on account of the hanging. It would give the men time to wet their whistle, maybe grab a hot bath and a shave and get a decent meal. More important, there was gonna be a free show, a saloon-woman named Dolores was due to be hanged. It seemed a customer had been a bit rough and she, waiting until he had passed out, had buried a knife in his throat.

'You done right, Walt,' Jack Jackson, his right-hand man advised. 'The men are getting down at heel, plumb worn out, for it has been a mighty long haul.'

Lock spat. 'It sure has. I reckon those varmints will get themselves as far as Galbraith and no further. The old-timer looked to be in a bad way, so they said, and the other varmint also.' He paused. 'I don't want no one excused. In our line of work a man needs a strong stomach. Watching that woman hang will toughen up the weaker ones. Hell, even the women of the town will be out and about in their bonnets and aprons to see the fun, but seeing a woman hang can affect younger men in peculiar ways.'

'Yep,' Jackson agreed. 'They are inclined to believe it ain't exactly right. It'll be done decent, so I hear. They will tie her skirts tightly around her ankles.'

Which was a pity, Lock thought, but wisely he kept such a reprehensible thought to himself. He was a respected law-enforcer, after all.

CHAPTER 5

He had buried his wife and infant daughter on the top of a high hill, a windswept, lonely place which Gertrude had liked to visit from time to time. She had liked to look out over the magnificent view of the rock-strewn landscape for miles around. Indeed, he and Gertrude had often joked about angry giants hurling rocks at whatever they spotted from the top of this very hill. This was the first time he had been here since her tragic death.

From his vantage place he spotted the circling buzzards and then two small objects far below. He came back to earth with a thud at this unwanted reminder that he was a lawman now, and unfortunately there was more to being a lawman than sitting in his office whittling away, carving wooden ducks. Or dodging Miz Jezabel! The thought sprang unbidden into his head and left him feeling mighty guilty for even thinking about that persistent woman. He was a widower after all!

Cussing, he began the trek downwards. A hunch told him that what he was going to come across was big trouble. But being a conscientious man he just could not avoid it.

The old man lay clutching his stomach, which was hurting him mighty bad, and the younger man lay unconscious whilst old Paul yelled at the buzzards to get on out of it. They were both done for and that was a fact. Lord, was that mean-hearted bastard Walt Lock destined to take their heads after all. Old Paul had seen them, or rather what remained, stuck on posts on the open range, warning wideloopers and troublemakers to keep on riding lest they got their just deserts.

Young Sam's horse had picked up a stone and his own horse had been run into the ground. Their luck was gone. Old Paul must have passed out; when he came round someone was wiping his face with a tepid cloth.

'Looks like your luck has run out, old-timer,' a quiet voice announced. 'You and your pard, but I am going to get you both into the town of Galbraith. There's a good woman there, Miz Gatrell. She'll care for you both as best she can. Yep! She makes a fine doc!'

Old Paul opened his eyes and the first thing he saw was the tin star. But this man, whoever he might be, was not Walt Lock and he was alone.

'We're done for!' Old Paul gasped. 'Sheriff Walt Lock is close behind.' With that he passed out again.

Naturally, Will had heard of Walt Lock. Gertrude had reckoned the man to be an absolute disgrace and certainly crazed. 'Well, I guess I am destined to meet him before too long.' Will muttered. He guessed he might have to lock horns with Walt Lock. Or maybe not! These two looked likely to die before Walt Lock arrived in Galbraith. No way was he going to hand live prisoners over to that lunatic.

'Lord, Will, are you purposely putting business my way?' Miss Gatrell observed with a sniff. 'I shall do my best but I don't hold out much hope.'

Will nodded. 'That's all anyone can do!' He was glad to get away. The sight of blood always tended to make him feel queasy. Indeed Gertrude had always had to do the butchering that needed doing from time to time out on a farm.

He was not surprised to find Bradley Worth hanging around outside the doc's place. Worth spat into the gutter as Will emerged. 'Lock is pure poison and he hates wrongdoers. He stamps on them hard and worse. Good old Walt Lock likes to bury wrong doers so that only their heads are left above ground. And, he likes to collect ears,' Worth declared without preamble. 'Fact is, he dries them out then strings them on his necklace.' He laughed heartily. 'You ain't going to try and emulate Walt Lock, are you, Pickle? You don't stand a hope in hell of measuring up to Lock.' He paused. 'I hear the hanging judge is on his way. What do you say?'

'Ain't you got work to do, Bradley? Every time I see you, you're idling around town.'

'That I am. That I am,' the gunslinger observed with a smirk. 'And it ain't by chance. Fact is Boss Parker has me here to keep an eye on what is going on. And I don't mind in the slightest, for sure as hell I find your antics amusing. But my boss does not. Fact is, I'm puzzled as to why I ain't been advised to take care of you.'

'Damned if I know and damned if I care,' Will replied with a shrug.

'You don't seem troubled by the possibility of crossing horns with Lock?' Worth essayed.

'Nope,' Will agreed.

'Nor hanging Mrs Benson!'

'Nope.' He moved away, whistling cheerfully. Worth frowned, things did not set right. He guessed they would find out tomorrow when the hanging judge arrived. He was also betting that sooner or later Boss Parker would have to make a move. One way or another Will Pickle had to be taken care of. The man would never learn to toe Boss Parker's line.

Judge Anthony Hickson was the sole passenger when the stage finally came to a bone-shaking stop in the town of Galbraith. Hickson was a man of some fifty-five years. He had a long, mournful face, world-weary, with prominent bags beneath his eyes which were a pale blue. His teeth were in pretty good shape and he prided himself both on his teeth and the fact that he had not mellowed with age. He had never once, despite the pleas of desperate men and their kin, been inclined to show mercy. Nor did he consider that a woman who had battered her husband to death with a hammer as he lay asleep deserved mercy. He was pleased to see, as he stepped down from the stage, that the good folk of this town had erected a scaffold.

Hickson headed for the hotel. His routine did not vary. He always took a long bath, then a good meal, and only then did he get around to the business of dealing out justice. The hotel would send word to the town council that he was here. An improvised court-room could be set up in the saloon, a jury of twelve good men selected and the business attended to. It was all a foregone conclusion. There was no defence.

In Galbraith, though, he soon discovered they did things a little differently.

'There is no help for it, Judge,' Michael Herman, the bank president, observed ruefully, 'We must hold the trial in the foyer of this hotel. Miz Jezabel has flatly refused to allow any kind of court to be set up in her saloon.'

The rancher Simon Parker nodded.

'What has the sheriff to say about this?' Judge Hickson exploded.

'Well actually, Judge, I would like a word concerning Sheriff Will Pickle,' Parker rejoined. 'After the trial, that is, for it is a delicate matter.'

Hickson nodded.

'We have two other wrongdoers in town,' Parker continued. 'But we will not concern ourselves with them, for I believe Sheriff Walt Lock will be here by and by to deal with them.'

'A good man, a good man,' Hickson agreed. 'Well, the hotel it is then. Gentlemen, shall we proceed with the business in hand?'

Gabe Benson watched them all trooping in. And those who were content to wait around outside for the hanging itself were taking opportunity to buy themselves a pie. It sure made Gabe feel sick. Fowles the restaurant proprietor was there, rubbing his hands and grinning foolishly. Gabe was overwhelmed with an urge to kill Fowles on account of that pie-table. A man had no business selling pies when he thought a woman was destined to hang. Gabe lounged on the sidewalk. No one knew who he was save the sheriff and two woman over at the saloon, Miz Jezabel and Miz Katy. He reckoned Sheriff Pickle must be sweet on Miz Jezabel. Pickle's ears turned red when he denied it. A sign, Gabe reckoned, that the sheriff was lying.

Dispassionately, Gabe decided he was gonna kill Fowles. That man was going to pay for selling pies. And as for the other two, Parker and Herman, sooner or later Will Pickle would be forced to deal with them. His money was on Pickle. He felt a kinship with the man, Pickle might not know it yet, but Pickle was not the inoffensive man he thought himself to be. Gabe reckoned that were Pickle to be set off the man would prove to be dynamite, totally unpredictable, of course. Why, Pickle might feel obliged to save Fowles from his just deserts. Now that presented a problem!

Will Pickle came out of the jail. Spotting Fowles he strolled over to the pie-table. 'This ain't the place for pies,' he observed. Seizing an edge of the tablecloth he gave a vicious jerk, sending the contents of the table down into the dirt. For good measure he stamped on them, pastry squashing beneath his boots which unfortunately soon became coated with juice and bits of well-stewed beef and potato.

'You're mad!' Fowles squealed.

'Damn varmint,' Will placed a palm against Fowles's portly frame and shoved, sending Fowles sprawling amongst his flattened pies.

Gabe Benson was ill-pleased to see folk commiserating with Fowles as they helped him up. Heads were nodded in agreement as Fowles loudly declared the sheriff must be mad.

'Bradley, take two of the men and fetch her over,' Parker ordered. 'And mind she don't bite, for she is clearly crazed.'

'You don't object then, Sheriff,' Bradley enquired quietly enough, but no one was fooled. He was more than ready to haul iron.

'Nope.' That this was not the expected response was clearly evident. Will kept a straight face. All hell was gonna break lose pretty damn soon, accusations would be hurled but there was not a damn thing anyone could do about it.

'Why, it is Mrs Parker,' Jezabel came through the batwings. 'Hanging around my saloon! So why are you here? To see Mrs Benson hauled out, I'll be bound. So why not step inside? Be my guest.'

'How dare you!' Mrs Parker recoiled. 'Have you no shame?'

'No. Have you?' Miz Jezabel winked. 'If you are seeking a job, why, let me tell you that that moustache you are sporting . . .'

'Excuse me, ladies.' Bradley Worth entered the saloon with a grin. He mounted the stairs two at a time, fully prepared to blast the door open. If the truth was told, he was enjoying himself. Lord, it was about time someone told Mrs Parker about that damn moustache!

His hand closed over the door-handle and the door opened with ease, causing Bradley to forget clean about Mrs Parker, for the room was empty.

'Where the hell is she!' He raced down stairs, nearly cannoning into one of the waddies who had accompanied him.

'Well, I am damned if I know,' Miz Jezabel replied, hands on ample hips as she surveyed him with a smirk, 'Fact is, Bradley, the door was left unlocked. An accident, of course. Miz Gatrell and Miz Cooper swear it was not them and I know it was not me but these things happen and . . .' But Bradley Worth was not listening; he was hot-footing it for the hotel.

'She's gone.' Bradley burst into the hotel foyer. 'One of those women left the door unlocked accidentally, so they say, not that anyone will admit to it.'

'Well, that's women for you,' Sheriff Pickle observed laconically.

'And you don't give a damn about it,' Simon Parker thundered. 'How long has she been gone? Get over there, Pickle. Bradley you organize a hunting party.'

'He is not the fool we think him to be,' Michael Herman cried. 'He has deliberately contrived to let her go free.'

'But why would I do that?' Will enquired.

'Because you ain't got the stomach to do your job,' Michael Herman responded furiously. 'Now get after

63

that woman!'

'Nope. Round up a few men and look for her yourself,' Will rejoined mildly.

'Bradley, take a few of the men and make a sweep around town for the woman. Herman, you take a few men and search the town. I reckon she is long gone but get at it anyway,' Simon Parker ordered curtly. He eyed Will Pickle. 'You're a joker, Will Pickle, and that is a fact! Don't think you are going to get away with this. We'll see who has the last laugh!'

'I reckon,' Will agreed with a degree of suspicion. Warning bells had sounded.

'Get going, Bradley,' Simon Parker bellowed, his voice vibrating with suppressed fury. 'And wipe that smile off your damn face.'

'I sure will boss. I sure will.' Bradley Worth swaggered out. 'This is your lucky day, Pickle, for I can best you any day!' he observed in an aside. But to his disappointment Will Pickle merely gave an offhand shrug.

Judge Hickson stood up. 'My time has been wasted. If you want a hanging find that woman and bring her back to face justice. I pronounce she is to be hung by the neck until dead. The trial is therefore concluded unless anyone wants to argue she is innocent.' No one spoke for a moment, then a chorus of: 'Hell, no, Judge,' broke out.

'Good day, gentlemen!'

Looking neither to right nor left Judge Hickson strode out of the foyer. Simon Parker followed close on the judge's heels. He was not displeased about how things had turned out because he knew just how he was going to get rid of Sheriff Will Pickle.

Gabe Benson watched as Bradley Worth and a handful of men rode out of town on what they all knew was a wild-goose chase. Sheriff Pickle had headed back to the jailhouse. Miz Jezabel, maybe just to outrage the respectable women of the town, was organizing what she called a horse-race. For a fee repectable men could get down on all fours and with saloon women on their backs crawl towards the finishing-post, a black ribbon tied to a stick set up by Miz Jezebel. There was free beer for anyone taking part. He spotted Miz Gatrell practically running towards the jailhouse, her skirt flapping around her ankles.

'Well, I did my best,' Miz Gatrell announced. 'Maybe if I had got them both sooner I could have saved them, but it was too late, Will, too late. Infection had set in, they had both bled considerably. Indeed it was a miracle they kept going for so long.'

'Well, that's the way it goes,' Will sighed. 'Fact is those two dying has saved me one heap of trouble. No way could I have stood aside and let this Walt Lock conduct lynching in my town. That man and myself would not have seen eye to eye. The late Mrs Pickle always reckoned Lock to be a crazy varmint.' He shrugged. 'Well, I guess we will see for ourselves by and by, for that varmint is sure to show up.'

'It looks like the Lord is watching out for you, Will,' she agreed, 'But I did my damnedest to save them even though it is better they died.'

He nodded. 'I know you did Miz Gatrell, and I would not have it any other way. Come tomorrow I will have that damn gallows dismantled.' He sighed. 'Bloodshed has been avoided today and for that I am grateful.'

Moses came in, a scowl upon his face. 'You ain't never to show your face in his restaurant ever again, so Fowles says, for you have shamed him before the eyes of the town.'

Will nodded. 'Well, that ain't a hardship, Moses. We have a stove here, after all. We must cook our food. How about a fried egg or two?'

'Well, I ain't hungry right now, maybe later. Say, did I ever tell you that I was the best ever when it came to roping a steer?'

'No. You never did.' Will tried to look interested as the old fellow droned on. Maybe it was true, maybe not.

'You don't believe me!' Moses accused.

'Hell, Moses! I never said that.'

A waddy poked his head round the jailhouse door. 'Fact is you are wanted over at the hotel. Boss Parker owes you some money. You ain't been paid in full!'

'Well, I can't rightly recall . . .' the oldster wheezed.

The waddy grinned. 'Never argue with the boss, Moses. If he says he owes you, then he owes you!'

Gabe Benson had idled in the town of Galbraith. The attraction had been Miz Katy. Also, not wanting to lock horns with Pickle he had decided to spare Fowles. He was in bed with Miz Katy, thankfully doing no more than smoking a cigar, when Miz Jezabel burst into the room without so much as knocking.

He sat up in some alarm cussing loudly; had the woman no decency, barging in without knocking, whilst Miz Katy wrapped herself in a blanket and clambered out of bed, concern written all over her face.

'What's wrong, Jez?' she exclaimed.

'Well, I am damned if I know,' Miz Jezabel rejoined. 'But something is wrong. I just know it and I reckon it's time, Gabe Benson, that you repaid the favour you owe Will Pickle, for it was his plan that saved your ma.'

Gabe stubbed out his cigar. *There was always a payback*, he reflected wearily. 'So Pickle is asking to be paid back!' he queried laconically.

'He ain't exactly asking,' Miz Jezabel replied. 'The fact is he's gone. I've noticed he ain't been around for a day or so and that old varmint Moses keeps telling me that Will left town on business, but I smell a goddamn rat. I know the old varmint is lying! Furthermore Herman is walking around grinning and Bradley Worth has been installed as our new lawman.' She snapped her fingers. 'Just like that. Will is gone and a replacement has been installed without anyone scarce noticing.' She paused for breath before continuing: 'That old blizzard Moses is involved in this. I've been around men long enough to know when something ain't right! There ain't been no gunplay but Will is gone. They've got the drop on him and that is a fact! Boss Parker has schemed and done for Will. But he ain't dead. I just know it. And now it is your duty, Gabe Benson, to ferret out the truth and set matters to rights.'

'You seem mighty worried, Miz Jezabel!' Gabe essayed.

'Well, it is true he ain't much to look at,' she conceded, 'but he's the only galoot who has ever turned me down. Hell, I just don't know why but I am so used to that varmint doing his damnedest to avoid me that I kind of miss him when I don't see him legging it in the opposite direction. I always keep a look out for him. He's given me an interest in life and now he ain't around. I want to know why. And if he needs help I reckon you're obligated, Gabe Benson, and that's a fact.'

Gabe clambered out of bed and pulled on his pants. 'We'll get the truth out of old Moses. If Will has been killed I'll blast the galoots who have done it. But we'll hope that ain't the case,' he added quickly, spotting the expression on Miz Jezabel's face. He buckled on his gunbelt before making his way down to the bar. He needed to grab Moses before those in the know, those responsible, realized that Moses needed to be silenced. Gabe was surprised that it had not already been done, for Moses was a loose end and that was a fact. And he was pretty damn sure that Bradley Worth would not put up with the smelly old coot bedding down in a jail cell.

CHAPTER 6

Bradley grabbed the oldster by his scrawny arm and pulled him forcibly from the jailhouse. 'You stink!' he accused, 'Lord, you ain't washed in days. Well, Pickle might not have been particular but I sure as hell am. You ain't staying in my jailhouse. Find yourself another roost, you old varmint.' With a forceful shove he sent Moses flying towards the sidewalk and on to Main Steet.

Moses picked himself up. 'After all I done, after all I done,' he stuttered in indignation.

'There's one thing that makes me want to puke,' Bradley rejoined, 'and that is a Judas! Get the hell out of my sight, you old bum!' He slammed the jail-house door in the old man's face.

'Come on, old-timer, come on.' Gabe, gripping old Moses by a scrawny arm, assisted him to his feet. 'I've got a jug you can share.'

'I ain't going anywhere near Miz Jezabel!' Moses had been drinking but still retained a few wits.

'Who said anything about that she devil. Back of the livery barn is where I stashed my jug.' Moses knew what had happened to Will Pickle and pretty damn soon he was gonna know too. Back of that livery barn was a high pile of manure. And Moses's face was gonna be pressed right into that mess until old Moses decided to spill the beans. Putting an arm around the old man's shoulders he steered him towards the stables.

'What the hell do you want?' the Scotsman, who owned the stables, demanded truculently.

'Get lost,' Gabe ordered. 'Fact is, I want the truth as to what has happened to Will Pickle.'

'A good man, a good man,' the Scotsman muttered.

Gabe steered a protesting Moses around the back of the barn. 'Best shut your mouth if you don't want a mouthful of dung,' he advised. 'Spill the beans and you can live. It's either that or be buried head first. What do you say?' With a forceful grip he pushed Moses down and on to the manure pile.

'Whatever they have promised you they won't deliver,' the Scotsman advised kindly, 'Why should they? You're nothing but an old varmint and no threat to anybody.'

'Grab a taste,' Gabe forced the oldster head down on the stinking dung.

As Gabe Benson rode by the Naked Lady saloon he lifted his hat. Miz Jezabel and Katy stared after him. The unspoken message was clear. He had discovered that which he needed to know.

As Gabe headed out of town he passed a group of dust-covered men riding in. He recognized the big red-headed galoot leading the hard-bitten crew into town, Sheriff Walt Lock, no less. And doubtless looking for trouble! But with Will Pickle well out of it there would be no trouble.

Walt Lock dismounted before the livery barn. There was some kind of fracas going on. One old-timer was cleaning up another old-timer who was plastered in manure and stinking to high heaven. But today Walt had no time to stop and enjoy the sight. He had no time for the old coots. 'See to our horses pronto,' Walt yelled. 'And I mean pronto or there is gonna be two old bums less in this world.'

'Yessir,' the more capable of the old-timers rejoined.

'Seen any strangers?' Walt enquired.

'No sir. I ain't seen no strangers but the town buried two dead ones a while back. Sheriff Pickle brought them in.'

'I'm gonna talk to your lawman!'

'Well we have a new man now: Bradley Worth.' The oldster paused. 'Word is Will Pickle has quit.' The livery man shrugged. 'Bradley Worth is your man.'

Bradley Worth came to his feet at the hammering on the door. Carefully he eased his Peacemaker out of its holster, not that he was expecting trouble although it was his intention by and by to call out the new gun in town. He always liked a challenge now and then. It kept him on his toes. He aimed to pick a fight with the gunman answering to the name of Gabe. And why not? The law was on his side.

Walt Lock came into the office. 'You know why I am here!' he stated without preamble.

Bradley Worth settled back in his chair. 'Feel free,' he offered, 'to dig 'em up if you have a mind to see them. Miz Gatrell done her best but they were done for in any event – wounds festering and all.'

'Much obliged.' Lock nodded. 'I'll dig 'em up just

to verify that they are the two varmints I've been after, but those varmints can wait until tomorrow. My boys deserve a good time. They have ridden long and hard.' He paused. 'Say, what happened to Pickle?' he enquired as an afterthought.

'He was out of his depth,' Bradley Worth rejoined. 'Sad to say the man went mad. He's been shipped out to an asylum but keep it to yourself. We don't want the town to know its lawman cracked up. It's bad for the image. A lawman has got to cope. It's expected. Pickle unfortunately proved himself a weakling.'

Walt Lock nodded. 'Yep. A sad day when a lawman cracks up. Well, I will see you around, Sheriff Worth.'

'Glad to have met you,' Bradley replied. He offered his hand and the two men shook on it.

Over at the livery barn Joe the Scotsman shook a fist at Moses. 'You damn fool. You ain't going to get your job back and you've been kicked out of the jailhouse. Now what are you gonna do!' He spat. 'Well, I reckon you can bed down in the barn. Leastways the horses won't be offended by the stink. But keep out of my way. You're a damn Judas and if Will Pickle ever gets back, well the Lord help you because no one else will!'

Will Pickle cursed himself for being a goddamn fool. His thoughts wandered as he recalled happier times.

'Well, not much happens to us,' his late wife used to say.

'Yep,' he would agree. 'One day is pretty much like another.' And that had been how they had wanted it to be. Neither of them had wanted any surprises or troublesome matters that had to be dealt with.

That no-good varmint Moses had been full of surprises! Will could not believe the oldster had bested him and brought him to this sorry predicament. He was being shipped to a lunatic asylum, destined to be buried without a trace amongst those deemed mad. Big-shot rancher Simon Parker had persuaded Judge Hickson to sign the papers. And Moses had lured Will to his doom. It had not taken much doing, for Will had been more than willing to humour the oldster.

Moses had prepared the groundwork well, rambling on about how he could not be beaten when it came to lassoing a steer or mustang and then, just to shut the oldster up, Will had agreed to witness a demonstration. They had moseyed on out of town to waste ground beyond the cemetery and there Moses, with practised ease, had lassoed Will and brought him down. As he had scrambled cussing to his feet Simon Parker, spurring his horse towards them had cast the second lasso. It had all been arranged, the collection cage had been sent for and indeed its driver and guard had been waiting in readiness for the collection. Himself!

'You have brought this on yourself.' Simon Parker had maintained a serious expression throughout, although Mike Herman had smirked away, clearly relishing this moment. 'It's clear as day that grief has deranged you. The crazy way you have carried on since pinning on your star confirms it.'

Old Moses, the Judas, had said nothing at all!

Shackled, Will lay in the cage. The two brutes in charge of him had already given him a thumping for speaking out. Playing up, they called it. His ribs hurt and he had lost a tooth. And now they were keeping him short of food, and water in particular.

'If you ain't deranged now you will be when you get to your destination,' one of them had promised with a guffaw.

Will reckoned they might be right. They had already passed through another town on their trek eastwards. Why, anyone would have thought a circus was coming town. Folk had come out to gawp and boys had taken it upon themselves to hurl stones and whatever refuse they could get hold of at Will's cage. And those two varmints in charge of him had found it all mighty amusing. They had actually warned Will to mind his manners and keep quiet or face another beating. He'd been left parked out in the searing heat whilst those two had taken their pleasure with the local floozies. The varmints were not in any hurry to get where they were going. And for that he supposed he ought to be thankful. He guessed things would only get worse once they incarcerated him behind asylum walls.

Bradley Worth watched as Walt Lock and his crew rode out. In a gunny sack hanging from his saddle were two heads. True to his word Lock had dug up the wrongdoers. And had then spent the night in hard drinking over at the Naked Lady.

'Drunken bums!' Miz Jezabel observed. She shrugged and turned to Katy. 'Maybe it is just as well Will ain't around at the moment. He never would have let them take those two heads.'

'More trouble coming,' Katy observed with a shrug, but Jezabel was no longer interested in what was going on at the jailhouse. Russell, who had spent the night at the saloon, then staggered out at break of day, was back.

'What the hell is it?' Worth demanded with displeasure. He also had spent the night at the Naked Lady. Walt Lock had been buying drinks all round. Now his head pounded and his eyelids were dropping. Whatever it was it was bad. Russell was bawling.

'Mrs Russell has had her throat cut from ear to ear and my girls are gone,' Russell gabbled. 'Damn renegades have got 'em.'

'You get yourself into the office. I'll get after Lock. Why, he'll skin those varmints alive once he gets hold of 'em.' Bradley lurched towards the livery barn. 'Joe, you good for nothing, get my horse saddled,' he bawled.

Joe hastened to oblige, thinking that with any luck Worth would fall out of the saddle and maybe break his neck.

'Rider coming fast.' Jack Jackson was the first to spot the dust cloud.

'Wait up,' Walt Lock ordered. 'Maybe we have trouble coming our way, maybe not.' He narrowed his eyes against the sun as he waited for the lone rider.

'Thank the Lord you are here,' Bradley yelled without preamble. 'You recall Russell, the big red-headed farmer, the one that dug up those two wrong-doers.'

'Yep. He dug them up for free beer. And that's what he got. I kept my word.'

'Well, it seems renegades have hit his farm. They've slit his wife's throat and taken his girls.'

'So!' Walt shrugged.

'Well, seems to me you're the man to get them, you and your crew.'

Lock thinned his lips. 'Galbraith ain't my town!' he stated coldly. 'My men have ridden long and hard. They've got families waiting for them, chores needing to be done and you're asking me to hit the trail again. Well, let me tell you, renegades steer clear of my town. They know what to expect. Why, we had ourselves a bonfire with two of them only last year!' He pointed a finger at Bradley Worth. 'You're the lawman of Galbraith. Round up a crew and get after them.'

Bradley bit back an angry retort. He had not signed on for law-keeping duties. His job was to see no one argued with Simon Parker and Mike Herman, who were planning to trap more two-bit ranchers and no-account farmers in debt. Boss Parker aimed to expand. He saw himself as a cattle baron and as such needed all the land he could get. Well, there was no help for it. Russell would just have to be told his kin were beyond help! There was going to be no damn posse.

Miz Jezabel was in the back parlour of her saloon. Men, she reflected, were bums with the exception of Will Pickle, who was a stubborn mule.

'Fact is,' Miz Katy was saying, 'you could say I am acquainted with the coyote that killed Russell's wife and took his girls. I nearly went upstairs with him one time.' She lit a cigar. 'But instinct told me to steer clear so, making up a pretext, I slipped out of the saloon. Doris went instead and the devil broke her neck. He calls himself Crazy Charles. Not Charlie mind but Charles – he is most insistent upon that. He is an Easterner, by the way, sent West by his family who paid him to leave. He's a mean, rotten, cruel varmint and worse than that he is quite mad. Lord! If anyone belongs in an asylum it's him.' She chewed her lips. 'The varmint hangs out a stone's throw from the border. He never raids in Mexico and it is an easy matter for him to slip over the border if needs be. Besides which there is a good market for taken women in those border towns.'

'How smart is he?' Jezabel asked. There was a certain expression on her face that Katy recognized.

'Very,' Katy replied quietly. 'He ain't smart to draw attention to himself but he possesses a natural cunning which has kept him alive,' she clarified.

Jezabel nodded. 'Since Will has gone certain varmints have been causing trouble down at the schoolhouse. They ain't quite sure Will ain't coming back so they ain't made a move yet. But they will. Varmints the lot of them.' She paused. 'And I'm gonna encourage them to do what is right. Keep quiet about what you know about Crazy Charles. We don't want those dogs turning on us when things go wrong.' She smiled. 'Strong liquor is called for, I believe!'

At the bar Russell was bawling into his glass of cheap rot-gut whiskey, as men took turns to commiserate.

'Drinks on the house!' Miz Jezabel yelled. 'You men drink as much as you need to ease the pain, especially you, Russell, for you are a good honest man and do not deserve to have this tragedy fall upon you.' She paused. 'Even you, Moses, you are welcome here.'

The old varmint she saw was wearing borrowed dungarees and a plaid shirt and was accompanied by Scotch Joe the livery man. Moses had already been at the jug, Jezabel guessed.

'Yah,' Moses yelled as he caught her eye. 'Will Pickle was never going to look at you, Miz Jezabel, for his late wife was a righteous woman. That is something you ain't!'

At this sally men began to laugh and Jezabel heard more than one crude comment. Even Russell, forgetting about his murdered wife and abducted daughters, could not refrain. 'Those varmints should have taken you, Miz Jezabel, and those harlots you employ and that is a fact.' His tone was ugly and she sensed danger.

'Drink up men.' She kept on smiling. 'Free liquor is what you deserve and it is the least I can do. I know you men will pursuade Worth to do what is right. I know you won't leave those poor girls to their fate.' She kept smiling. 'They are respectable womenfolk after all, not saloon floozies. Ain't that so, Joe.'

'It sure is, Miz Jezabel,' Joe yelled. 'And if Bradley Worth is a better man than Will Pickle he won't give them up for lost.'

'And there ain't no doubt he is a better man,' Miz Katy encouraged.

The two women retreated into the parlour. All they had to do now was wait. Joe could be trusted to fan the flames. Like it or not Bradley Worth was going to lead a posse in pursuit of Crazy Charles. Both women hoped that posse would fare badly.

'I'll be making a move pretty damn soon,' Simon

Parker confided. He sat across the table from Bradley Worth. Both men were smoking cigars. 'There are one or two who won't sell up. Now those men found with my butchered steers on their land are to be given a choice. They sell up. They take what I am offering and head out or else stand trial for rustling. You make it plain that rustling is a hanging offence. We do things plain and simple and we cannot go wrong. You find the evidence, Bradley, and give them the choice. You can deputize half a dozen of the crew. You'll need back-up.' He paused, 'Naturally I'm gonna make it worth your while.'

'Yessir,' Bradley agreed with a smirk. 'I take it I will be looking at a sizeable bonus!'

'Indeed,' Simon Parker agreed. Will Pickle would never have agreed to any of this. The former sheriff, by his mule-headed foolishness, had brought misfortune upon himself.

The door opened to admit Mike Herman. 'That damn fool woman has given the men free booze!' he declared. 'As much whiskey as they can stomach – and that is plenty!'

'So!' Bradley gave a shrug.

'Practically the whole damn town is marching on the jailhouse!'

'What the hell!' Bradley could hear the commotion.

'You ain't going to be able to stop them. They have waddies from outlying ranches among them, even some of your men, Simon. They are all of them drunk, all of them demanding Bradley save the girls. They want to see the varmints who took them skinned.'

Stones thudded against the door and windows of the jailhouse. Glass shattered. 'Will Pickle might have been loco,' a voice yelled, 'but the varmint would have gone on after them.'

'You ain't fit to fill his boots!'

Bradley came to his feet with a curse. He aimed to blast the speaker.

'No need for threats,' a voice yelled. 'Bradley Worth is twice the man Pickle was. He'll do right. He'll save the womenfolk. He'll exact vengeance.'

'Damnation,' Bradley muttered, aware that he was being backed into a corner. Even absent, Pickle caused trouble.

'There ain't nothing for it.' Simon Parker took decisive action. 'I need the town with us. Bradley, fact is you have got to swear in a posse. Townsfolk will do. And you must make a show of looking for them girls. Only when the going gets tough will those polecats want to call it a day. And then you shepherd them back to town.'

'Hell, I don't like it. If you had waited a while before ousting Pickle it would have been more to my liking. That mule head was fool enough to go after them solo!' Bradley spat. 'And now I've got the job.' For a moment he considered removing his star and thumping it down on the desk. 'I am losing face here!' he snarled. 'Those no-account bums will think they have forced my hand.'

He stomped out of the jailhouse to confront the town. 'So you have rounded up the men, have you, Russell? Good, good, all I was waiting on were good men to ride with me. And here they are. We'll get your girls back and we'll skin the varmints that took them.' He scarcely paused. 'You men that are going to ride with me, get yourselves coffee, stick your heads in the horse-trough, for I cannot take any that cannot sit a saddle. Russell, you come with me. We'll organize the victuals and ammo. We'll find your girls, never fear.'

Walt Lock watched as the sheriff of Galbraith rode away. 'Damn bastard,' he observed. 'He's one of those varmints who ain't particular when it comes to upholding the law.'

It had soon become apparent to Gabe Benson that the two varmints in charge of luckless Will Pickle were not in any hurry to get back to their asylum. Every chance they got the two were stopping to swill liquor and enjoy any woman prepared to sell her favours. And that was all to the good, Gabe reflected. They were done for in any event. He'd have to kill them to prevent them squealing after Will had been sprung. And if Will had any sense he would keep on riding and never head back to Galbraith. But he guessed that Will Pickle lacked sense. There was going to be a reckoning in the town of Galbraith.

CHAPTER 7

Russell burst into tears as he pointed at the crude lettering burnt into the wood of his door. WELCOME HOME it read. The renegades had taken time out to leave a message. 'I ain't touched the missus,' he groaned. 'I let her be.'

'We'll get 'em!' a farmer bellowed. 'Those varmints are going to pay!'

Bradley Worth eyed the remains of Mrs Russell. She'd been tied on to her rocking-chair and then, by the look of it, her throat had been cut. Her blood-soaked knitting still lay upon her lap. Dried blood had congealed and flies buzzed around, sometimes settling upon the woman.

'Well, now that you have seen her, Sheriff, are you agreed that she must be buried forthwith?' someone asked.

'Of course, of course,' Bradley agreed, anything to delay the manhunt. 'And we'll say a few words, we'll do this right.' That ought to delay them further.

'What kind of animals could have done this?' John Wolf, a quietly spoken farmer asked as he took up a spade.

'Well, he has left his handle. He calls himself Charles,' Bradley observed with a frown. 'Men, it seems to me we are hunting a renegade known as Crazy Charles!'

'Well let's get after them!' Russell yelled, 'John Wolf, you dig the grave and bury my wife and then you come on after us. We've got to find my girls . . .' Breaking down again, he was unable to continue.

Bradley Worth nodded. 'Mount up, let's ride, let's go get them.' Loud cries of approval greeted his words. 'Russell, you are a fair hand at tracking, so I have heard.' Russell, he guessed, was the worst of them when it came to tracking. Bradley had no intention of catching up with the renegades. He guessed they were over the border right now. That suited him real fine.

John Wolf began to dig. The sooner she was buried the sooner he could set out after them. His stomach heaved at the sight of poor Mrs Russell and as the hunting party disappeared from sight the young farmer spewed his guts, then adjusted his bandanna in a fruitless attempt to keep the grit and dust from his nostrils. It was going to be one hell of a day, he reflected, striking the earth savagely, imagining his shovel thudding into the evil monster responsible for this outrage.

Shackled as he was, Will Pickle could not even raise his bandanna to protect himself from the hot and gritty wind that was blowing across the land. His eyes were almost closed. His tormentors had handed out another beating last night when they had made camp. By now he was almost hearing voices, voices carried by the wind, *a good day to die* they whispered. He must be going mad, he thought. And why not! He was done for. He was a goner.

'What the hell have we here?' Above the howl of the wind he heard the voice of one of his tormentors, the fat one, the one whom, for want of a name, he thought of as Fatso. The son of a bitch stank like a pig and ate like one, shovelling huge amounts of food into his mouth, burping and slurping as he guzzled. The wagon came to an abrupt halt.

'Seems like this pilgrim's luck has run out,' Gregg, Fatso's partner rejoined. It seemed likely that Fatso was going to investigate what they had here! Gregg always had something wrong with him. The complaints varied. Sometimes he felt dizzy. Other times his legs would be about to give way. Why, he could scarcely breathe or stand, he would croak. And as for his boots, why, they were pinching real bad! All these afflictions had not hindered him when he had set about giving Will a good kicking yesterday evening.

Will hated the pair with a vengeance. The two varmints knew damn well what they were doing. Furthermore they were enjoying what they were doing.

Fatso, whose handle was Bill Bratton, descended from the wagon with a grunt. Blood had pooled beneath the still form that lay face downwards, motionless and not long dead. Which meant that whoever had blasted him could still be around. Bratton glanced round. There was nowhere hereabouts for anyone to hide; the land was bare, the vegetation sparse. Or maybe the pilgrim had made it here from someplace else. Tumbled from his horse which had also made itself scarce, and here he lay.

'I feel kind of dizzy,' Gregg whinged. 'Check him out will you, and then perhaps we can get on. We've got a woman to collect, remember?'

'I sure do,' Bratton rejoined. He laughed. 'Let's hope she is young and pretty.'

'You can say that again.' Gregg grunted. He scratched his bald head. 'They don't do well, removed from company.'

'What the hell are you talking about?' Bratton moved towards the corpse.

'Well, I mean to say, this lunatic here.' Gregg jerked a thumb towards Will Pickle. 'He's a rarity. We mostly get women to collect. Seems they crack easier. The solitude of frontier life turns them crazy.'

'Yep. And I ain't complaining.' Bratton leered, bending down to turn the corpse over. It was his intention to check for a money-belt.

The worst of it had been the flies, Gabe Benson reflected. They had troubled him badly. But he had timed it well. It had been an easy matter getting in front of these two varmints, waylaying them if they had but known it. He knew all about the varmints. They'd boasted plenty in the saloons they favoured about how they dealt with their charges. Why, he was doing the world a service, Gabe reflected, as he waited for the feel of a hand upon his shoulder.

'Let's see what we've got,' Bratton grunted, instincts that ought to have told him something was wrong kicking in a mite too late.

Gabe came rolling to his feet with the speed and agility that only the young possessed. In the process his booted foot hit the fat man fair and square in the mouth, sending him backwards with a howl of pain.

'Freeze,' Gabe yelled, and Gregg, who had been about to reach for his rifle which rested behind him rather than beside him, froze.

Will Pickle forced his eyelids open. He recognized that voice. Gabe Benson, of all people! Well, it figured. Benson was a man who paid his debts, good or bad.

Bill Bratton lurched to his feet.

'Me and Will Pickle have unfinished business,' Gabe told him conversationally. 'I ain't going to harm you.'

'Why didn't you say,' Gregg grumbled. 'We would have handed him over without protest. There ain't need for violence.'

'No, there ain't. Bratton, you unbutton your gunbelt real slow. And you Gregg, get down from the wagon. Don't make the mistake of trying to take up your rifle. You won't make it.'

Bratton wondered whether they could get the better of this man. If they did, well, he would know it. No one kicked Bill Bratton in the mouth and got away with it.

'Get that cage unlocked and then get Pickle out of it. And get them shackles off him,' Gabe yelled. 'Pronto or my finger may just squeeze this trigger. I ain't a patient man.'

'Yessir.' Gregg was anxious to comply. For once his complaints did not seem to be troubling him.

'Get inside the cage yourselves,' Gabe bellowed. 'I need to settle with Pickle. Now I ain't going to harm either one of you and that is a fact,' he reiterated.

Hell, he had almost forgotten their boots. 'Get your boots off real slow. You don't look like men who would be handy with a blade but I've got to sure you ain't carrying one.' Gabe himself had a blade concealed in his boot.

'Back away from the door.' He turned the key. And there they were, Will's tormentors locked inside the cage used to transport the poor unfortunates deemed lunatics but no doubt as sane as anyone else out and about on the frontier.

Will lay flat out on the ground. Kneeling, Gabe trickled tepid water over Will's parched lips. 'Well,' he drawled, 'I guess you ain't in any condition to decide what to do with these two varmints. No sir.' Whistling, Gabe began to unfasten the unfortunate critters assigned to pull the wagon. The horses were slow, he reflected, but strong. Loading Will Pickle over the back of one of them Gabe, still whistling, leading both horses began to walk away.

Howls erupted in his wake. He was leaving them to certain death.

Crazy Charles counted on the fact that very few *hombres* were reckless enough to pursue him. And of those that did, well, he liked to set an example to deter others. Walt Lock would have been one hell of a challenge but Charles had avoided any prospect of confrontation with Lock by keeping well clear of territory where Lock was the law.

Charles had found that whereas enraged ranchers would bond together to set out after wideloopers, women were another matter, especially ones who belonged to poor farming folk. In general the community tended to write them off as lost. But if they didn't Charles knew just how to deal with anyone who came after him. He flourished because of his ability to generate fear. If there were men out hunting him Charles preferred to deal with them sooner rather than later. He had never been a man who cared to look over his shoulder.

Bradley Worth was no fool and it was not long before he realized that the galoots they were following were making no attempt to hide their tracks. This fact naturally set alarm bells ringing. Russell was tracking them with ease. This was all wrong and Bradley aimed to get out.

'It's clear to me they are laying a false trail,' he announced after calling a halt.

'Well it ain't clear to me!' Russell oozed belligerence.

Bradley ignored the farmer. 'I feel obliged to circle round and see if I can pick up the genuine article. You men wait for me here.' He adjusted his bandanna. The damn grit was flying everywhere.

'You ain't quitting on us,' Russell growled. 'We need you. We need a fast gun, a man who can shoot straight.'

'Lead on then, if you are convinced we're on the trail,' Bradley yelled. 'Lead on. I will be happy to follow. But I tell you we have been led a dance!'

'It's agreed then. We stick together,' Russell growled.

'Yep, it's agreed.'

Taking the words at face value Russell took the lead, the others falling in behind. Bradley thinned his

88

lips. Charles had left a trail that even these dumb farmers could follow. They were being led into a trap. Bradley fell back until he was at the rear of the bunch, allowing the distance between himself and the bunched riders to lengthen slowly. He intended to fork it out real quick. But he must choose his time carefully. Many of the farmers were good shots when it came to using rifles. Backs presented a broad target.

Charles had always found that folk tended to behave in a predictable way. He often used this to his advantage. The bereaved, he knew, seldom thought straight. That he was being followed he knew for he had posted look-outs on higher ground. When the signal came, a flash of sunlight on glass, he put his plan into action. It was very simple. He intended to ambush his pursuers whilst they were momentarily distracted.

Unfortunately the distraction had to be one of the girls. Nothing else would throw them all into temporary confusion. He decided upon the scrawny one because he had noted that plump females always sold best. It was all over very quickly, he snapped her neck with a forceful twist before she even realized what he intended to do. The other two, who were gagged and bound, went crazy but, given their condition, were no trouble.

Primed by Charles what to expect, his men were mounting, stamping out the camp-fire and getting ready to move out, to take up their assigned positions. Crazy Charles lit a cigar. It was all coming together. He truly believed he was unstoppable.

Russell, who was in the lead, saw her first as they rounded a bend in the trail. Besides the remains of a dead fire lay a small shape wearing what had once been a bright-yellow dress. It was Rebecca, his youngest. Uttering a bellow of grief the distraught father spurred his horse, practically throwing himself from the saddle when he reached his daughter. And the rest of the men followed suit.

Bradley seized his chance. This was the moment to fork it out. As the bullet that hit him mid-chest knocked him from the saddle his mind registered in the last second of life that he had left it too damn late to make his move.

His horse bolted and Bradey, foot still caught in the stirrup, was dragged in the terrified animal's wake as all hell broke lose. Ambushed men, slow-thinking farmers were shot down like sitting ducks.

John Wolf was not much of a tracker. He felt uneasy out in the wilderness alone. In fact he was plain terrified. The only place he wanted to be was his farm, his patch of land where he felt at home. Out here his stomach churned and, as he had feared, he somehow took a wrong turn. Some time had elapsed before he realized his mistake and painstakingly back-tracked. John began to worry that this delay in catching up might cause the others to believe that he had a yellow streak. He had been raised to believe that men could not admit to fear and this thought caused him considerable grief.

Ever practical, John travelled slowly, noting down markers, odd-shaped rock configurations, stunted bushes, anything which could be used as some kind of a map should he have to get himself back to town solo.

It was with some relief that he spotted the lone

horse standing quietly, reins dangling, some distance before him. The relief dissipated as he quickly realized that the animal had run itself into the ground and worse, it was the horse that had belonged to Sheriff Bradley Worth. And there were, he noted with considerable alarm, circling buzzards on the horizon.

Every inclination told him to get the hell out of here. Somehow he managed to squash these shameful promptings. Sweat trickling down his face and his body, the smell of fear enveloping him, he forced himself to proceed. It did not take him long to find the lump of red meat that had been Sheriff Bradley Worth. Bloodstained heads and necks wobbling, squawking their protest the buzzards retreated at his approach.

'Lord help me,' John muttered, 'Lord help me.' He left the pitiful remains of the sheriff and rode on for there were more circling buzzards up ahead. He didn't need any tracking skill to find the remains of the posse. They were dead, every goddamn last one of them. He clutched the horn of his saddle. Tears ran down his face. The ones who had died outright had been the ones the Lord had spared. The others who had not been spared had suffered terribly. Russell had been beheaded and the head must have been taken for he could not see it anywhere. And two others had been roasted, tied to spits and placed over fires. The stench of burnt flesh seemed to linger still and flies were everywhere. John knew this dreadful sight would be with him until his dying day, which could even be today if he did not fork it back to the town of Galbraith pretty damn quick.

*

Gabe Benson had found a place to hole up. He had found the deserted sodbusters' cabin before he had chosen his spot to ambush the tumbleweed wagon. A well had been sunk and there was blackish water at the bottom, enough for the two of them and the horses. Not wanting to come down with stomach cramps he took particular care to boil the drinking water before lighting up a cigar. He resigned himself to staying here until Will Pickle had regained some degree of strength. Pickle was now racked with fever, babbling away about his late wife Gertrude and, on occasion, Pickle had even yelled out Miz Jezabel's name.

Gabe set about cooking up a thin stew made from a scrawny bird he had potted. He would see Pickle upon his feet and fit to ride and after that Gabe was forking it out. Pickle was on his own. And that was exactly how Will Pickle would expect things to be. Pickle was a man he could respect. The only thing he had done wrong was to trust that lying old Judas, Moses. Why, the man ought to be pegged out to dry in the sun, and had Gabe been in Will's old boots why, he guessed he would do it.

There was no doubt in Gabe's mind that Pickle would be returning to Galbraith. Miz Jezabel was there for one thing. And doubtless Pickle would want revenge upon Herman and Parker. And Bradley Worth would need to be blasted. But these were matters which did not concern Gable. Maybe he ought to track down the hanging judge, the one who would have hanged his ma, the one who had committed Will to an asylum. Yep, maybe he ought to track him down and slit his throat. As Gabe spooned stew down an almost unconscious Will Pickle he contemplated this idea.

Will sat up right with a howl of pain. Gertrude had just passed over. Miz Gatrell, who had been at the birth had gazed at him with tears in her eyes.

'I am sorry, Will,' she had sobbed. 'I did my best but they are both gone.'

'Leave me, Miz Gatrell,' he had said. When she had gone he had howled like a dog driven mad with grief. He remembered it all clearly.

'So you are back in the land of the living,' a voice drawled.

'Gabe!' he croaked. He was remembering other events now. He remembered pinning on that damn star, and look where he had ended.

'Yep, sent after you by Miz Jezabel! We're quits now. I am heading out!'

'Thank you kindly, Gabe,' Will croaked. 'And take care. Go look up your ma. Set your gun aside.'

'And you go look up old Moses. And take care you do not set your gun aside, for he is a treacherous varmint.'

'As are the rest of them,' Will rejoined grimly. One way or another there was going to be one hell of a reckoning. He felt kind of glad Miz Jezabel had cared enough to send Gabe Benson after him.

'Hell, I would have come after you anyway,' Gabe declared as if guessing his thoughts. I am a man who always settles his debts one way or another.' Yep, and before he left the territory he aimed to settle with the hanging judge.

CHAPTER 8

'So long!' Gabe Benson mounted his horse and rode away. He did not look back.

Will hauled himself into the saddle, doing his best to ignore the pain. He was still bruised and stiff thanks to Fatso and Gregg. But he guessed that by now his former tormentors would be two maggot infested lumps that had once called themselves men. Well, he did not give a damn about either of them. They had been given their just deserts, no doubt about it. Those two had not deserved a merciful end.

He headed back towards the town of Galbraith and the unfinished business that awaited him. He was annoyed to find Miz Jezabel filled his thoughts, rather than the matter in hand – exacting vengeance! She was one hell of a woman, he had to admit, but he was a widower, after all, and he felt guilty just even allowing himself to think about her. He sighed. He needed a sign, a sign to tell him Gertrude would have approved. But this was fanciful thinking and he was not a fanciful man.

*

The commotion on Main Street, clearly audible inside the Naked Lady saloon, brought Miz Jezabel flying downstairs, hopeful that Will Pickle might have returned. She practically threw herself through the batwings, red hair in disarray, wearing only her night attire, her face bereft of powder and her eyes heavy with sleep. She did not look her best but she did not give a damn.

'Goddamnit,' she muttered, annoyed to see it was only young John Wolf causing the commotion. And what a commotion it was. The young farmer was gesticulating wildly. He was a dust-covered figure, almost collapsed and in need of physical support from his fellows.

'They are done for, Miz Jezabel, the whole darn bunch of them, Bradley Worth included,' a customer whose name she could not immediately recall informed her.

'You don't say!'

'I do say.' He proceeded to spill the beans as to what had occurred before adding hopefully: 'Any chance of a free whiskey? I sure as hell need it.'

She hesitated, her first inclination to tell him to go to hell, but she, after all, had encouraged the men to set out after the raiders, hopeful that things would go wrong, and all because those varmints were causing trouble at the schoolhouse, self-righteously declaring that the young ones from the saloon had to be excluded. But no one would remember. 'Sure,' she replied. 'Free drinks for those who need it. I am damn sorry this has come to pass,' she lied. Leastways Will Pickle had been well out of it when this trouble blew up, for that fool man was crazy enough to set out after the renegades solo. Will might have ended up being roasted on a spit. The possibility did not bear thinking about. Why, she felt obliged to retire to her parlour and lie down.

Will did not head directly for town. He headed back towards his old farm, the place he had known during his happiest times. He had decided he needed the Peacemakers that he felt comfortable using. Gertrude's pa had bequeathed him a gunbelt and two Colt .45s. Will had never worn them, for there was blood on those guns theoretically speaking. The old man had not kept a count of the men he had blasted, for there had been too many to remember.

The old man had never liked Will but had decided to leave him the guns anyway, as there was no one else and his father-in-law had wanted the weapons kept in the family. 'My Gertrude is more fitted to wearing them than you, Will Pickle,' he had jibed more than once, but Will had merely shrugged. 'I reckon,' he had always agreed. It had become a family joke.

Well, he reflected grimly as he dismounted alongside the old dead tree in whose hollowed trunk these weapons had been concealed, the time for joking was long gone. Lightning had struck this tree in its prime and turned it into an empty husk. The hollow trunk had made a mighty fine hiding-place for the guns, carefully wrapped and tended throughout the years just in case they were ever needed. Now they were! The wearing of them would make a statement that he hoped folk would heed.

He unwrapped the guns and slid them into the holsters. He would have ridden away there and then but angry voices halted him in his tracks. Two waddies, Simon Parker's men, were emerging from the farmhouse, clearly they had seen him and had taken exception to what they saw. He waited patiently, knowing he had little choice but to play the cards as they fell.

'He's back!' the older of the two bellowed. 'That goddamn crazy bastard is back.'

'He sure is.' The two advanced, inane grins on their faces. 'Mr Parker ain't going to like this. He leaves express instructions that when he runs no-account bums off property they ain't been able to keep, if any of those no-account bums is so foolish to show his face again they get blasted.'

Will hadn't known this. Parker, after all, was new to the territory and had just begun acquiring land with the collusion of smooth-talking Mike Herman.

'Well gents, you would be very foolish indeed to listen to what Boss Parker says,' he warned them quietly.

'You crazy dog,' the older man yelled. 'You've come back sniffing around where you ain't wanted and now you are going to face the consequences.' He paused. 'Say, where the hell did you get those guns?'

'They belong to me,' Will replied calmly. He could see what was coming. 'I can use them real well.'

'You damn liar, Will Pickle. You ain't going to talk your way out of this. You're a dead man.' They both reached for their shooters, meaning to fill him full of holes before he went down in the dirt.

He was ahead of them, and already reaching for the Colts even before the words *dead man* had left the fool's lips. The guns slid from the holsters with practised ease. Hell, he'd always practised over the years, just in case he'd needed to defend Gertrude and the farm! His finger closed over the triggers before the other two had cleared leather. Dispassionately he squeezed the triggers. They went down, one hit fair and square mid-chest, the other with his head blown away.

He had changed, he reflected. There was no desire to vomit. He felt nothing at all. And before he headed on into Galbraith he was going into the farmhouse to brew himself a mug of coffee. And maybe get himself a hot meal. And as for those two fools, they could lie where they had fallen, a lure for the flies and maggots which followed in the wake of death. Sure as hell he was not going to bury them nor tote them into town for burial. He'd best turn their horses loose, he decided. No need for them to suffer. No doubt by and by someone would eventually check up on the missing men.

He rode into Galbraith. The first thing to be done was to blast Bradley Worth, the town's new sheriff That had to be got out of way. The two of them were on collision course. One of them had to die.

'Will Pickle, Will Pickle,' a voice yelled out. He would have reached for his gun had he not recognized the lingering Scottish tones of Joe the livery man. 'All hell has broken loose,' Joe cried. 'Come on into the barn and I'll fill you in. You need to know.'

'I need to blast Bradley Worth.'

'Well that you can't do. He's gone, reduced to raw meat, shot and dragged by his horse, a terrible sight, so young John Wolf declares.'

'What the hell has John Wolf got to do with Bradley Worth?' Wary of a trap, Will swung down from the saddle and followed Joe cautiously into the barn. The first sign that things were not right he aimed to shoot first and ask questions later.

The first sight which greeted him was Moses, lying unconscious in an empty stall spread-eagled on the straw, clothes filthy, stinking of whiskey as he snored away, dead to the world.

'Well, there he is if you want to blast him,' Joe advised.

'You brought me in here for that?' Will snapped.

'Hell no. But you need to know what has gone down in your absence.'

Will shrugged. 'Spill the beans.'

Relishing the attention Joe spilled the beans. 'So in an odd kind of way you've been spared one rotten can of worms,' Joe concluded.

'Goddamnit!' Will exclaimed. He knew he had no choice. He had to go after the two surviving Russell girls. He had to fetch them back to Galbraith. And he would have to kill Crazy Charles as well. Because if he did not the man would come looking for him, intent on vengeance because Will had interfered in this profitable matter. The girls no doubt had been sold and were over the border by now.

'So what do you aim to do,' Joe was asking but he was referring to Moses not the Russell girls.

'I aim to do what's right,' Will rejoined. 'Go get a bucket of water.' He roused Moses by dousing him with water. Squawking like a chicken the oldster propped himself into a sitting position. 'I ain't got time for you right now,' Will told him, 'Get on over to the jailhouse, get cleaned up and put tea to brew.'

'You ain't going to blast him?' Joe observed incredulously.

'Nope. He's been taken for a fool by big-shot Parker. He knows it. That's punishment enough for a man like Moses, for he came into this territory with Parker. I reckon he has devoted years to toiling for Parker. Well, now he knows they counted for nothing. Now get over to the jailhouse, Moses. I aim to forget about your one mistake.'

'But . . .' Joe began, falling silent when he saw Will Pickle heading for the door, no doubt heading for the saloon and Miz Jezabel.

But Joe was wrong. Will headed for the bank and Mike Herman. The place was empty except for the half-asleep clerk dozing behind the counter. Upon seeing Will the man jumped to his feet and gave Will a goggle-eyed stare.

'Have the day off and you can tell Herman I said so,' Will declared. The clerk scuttled out without a backward glance, glad to be away from the trouble that was surely going to erupt. Will drew his Peacemaker and came through the door gun in hand.

'Pickle!' Mike Herman froze with fright.

Will wanted to gun him down real bad, but fought the urge. He was taking back his town and as a lawman he could not follow his own inclinations. He could only blast those who brought it upon themselves by hauling iron. Clearly Herman was not going to haul iron.

'You and me are moseying over to the saloon. And you are going to tell the whole damn bunch of them that the order committing me to an asylum was forged. I don't reckon the hanging judge will be around to contradict you.'

'You've killed him!'

'Nope. But he ain't going to be around. Now, what's it to be? You do as I say or I blast you where you sit? I reckon I will need to do it sooner or later.'

'What if I do as you ask?' Herman was trying to bargain.

'Well, it's up to you. I'll treat you the same as the rest of the varmints in this town. Step out of line and I'll blast you. Toe the line and I will leave you be. And that means severing your partnership with Parker. He ain't taking over no more foreclosed farms. I know how he operates now. And it ain't right. Why, I myself have recently gunned down two of his hirelings. Forced to do it to save my skin. I am sure you understand.'

Herman nodded. Simon Parker would be forced to have Pickle blasted now in any event. The man's return was a temporary set-back, nothing more.

'And I need a considerable sum, donated by your bank. I aim to buy those two girls back, it being best for them that this matter be concluded as quickly as possible.'

'Will Pickle!' Miz Katy screamed as he came

through the batwings, Mike Herman walking just a little way before him.

'Where's Miz Jezabel?'

'In her parlour, lying down.'

'Don't disturb us! It's drinks all round courtesy of Herman but first he has something to say. Ain't that right, Mike?'

From the corner of his eye Mike spotted Missouri, a waddy who rode for Parker, heading for the batwings. The man was off to inform his boss that Will Pickle was back in town. Pickle was destined to learn pretty soon that he had made one hell of a mistake in coming back to Galbraith.

'Thank the Lord you are safe,' Miz Jezabel cried, flying up, grabbing Will and pulling him down on to the sofa. All coherent thoughts flew out of his head and it was some considerable time before he got around to voicing the reasons that had brought him into the parlour.

Miz Jezbal sighed. 'I knew I would get you in the end, Will Pickle.'

'That's as maybe, Miz Jezabel,' he replied. 'And thank you kindly, but I am obliged to fork it out pretty damn quick.'

'Simon Parker. . . ?' she essayed.

'Simon Parker be damned, Miz Jezabel. Why, I am duty bound to set out after the Russell girls and return them to Galbraith as soon as I can. I reckon they will be over the border and sold by now. Crazy Charles can wait. I need to retrieve the girls first.' He paused, there was an odd expression on her face. 'I'd be obliged, Miz Jezabel, for any suggestions as to where I might look. What kind of scum buys stolen women. If you could come up with a list of possible places I'd have somewhere to start.'

Miz Katy, who had been listening outside the parlour door, her ear catching a muffled endearment from time to time, jumped back as Miz Jezabel lost her temper.

'It ain't nothing to do with you, Will Pickle!'

'But I am a lawman, Miz Jezabel.'

There was the sound of smashing china. and more considerable screeching from Miz Jezabel, followed by a list of profanities directed at Will Pickle.

Her temper was fearsome to see, Wiil thought, as he dodged a flying vase – but not quickly enough, for a shard cut him on the temple causing a trickle of blood to run down his cheek.

Miz Jezabel stopped as abruptly as she had started. She had done it now, driven him away for ever. 'I'd be obliged for that list,' he said as if nothing had happened.

'You're done for, Will Pickle, but why should I care? I'll write you out a list.'

'Thank you kindly, Miz Jezabel.'

'Don't thank me. I ain't doing you a favour. You're bent on self-destruction and that's a fact.'

Missouri came into Simon Parker's study without knocking. A string of profanities left Parker's lips.

'He's back!' Missouri yelled, interrupting the flow. 'Will Pickle is back as large as life.' Missouri hesitated. 'A riderless horse has just come in. It belongs to Burke.'

'Burke?'

'You put him to keep an eye on Pickle's old place.'

'He's been there all this time?'

'Well, you never pulled him out of there.'

Simon Parker got to his feet. 'Round up the men. I am going to settle with Pickle once and for all. As far as I am concerned he is a runaway lunatic, a danger to himself and others, a mad dog that does not deserve any kind of consideration.' First they would swing by the Pickle spread. He wanted his men to see what was there. Burke was dead, to be sure, gunned down by Pickle who had clearly crossed the line. And how the hell had he got out of the tumble-weed wagon transporting him to an asylum?

The thought nagged away at him. There was only one man to blame for this mess. That man was Mike Herman, the practical joker. If Herman had kept his mouth shut Pickle would have ridden out, quit the territory for good because there was nothing to keep him here. Without his wife and child the farm had meant nothing to the man. And that idiot Herman had contrived to keep Pickle around, gone out of his way to do it, conjuring up a job that Pickle had not even been seeking.

Simon Parker led his men into Galbraith. The town looked as normal. Respectable womenfolk were going about their business, Scotch Joe was dozing outside his livery barn as usual, George Green was open for business. Green would have closed up at the prospect of gunplay, for the man was an out-and-out coward. Across Main Street he saw Moses shuffling out of the bathhouse cleaned up, wearing faded dungarees too big for his scrawny frame, a handout no doubt.

'Where the hell is Pickle?' Parker yelled without preamble.

'Try the saloon.' Moses cackled, knowing damn well that Will had ridden out.

Simon Parker brought his men to a halt before the Naked Lady saloon. Taking the lead he burst through the batwings. Miz Jezabel in all her finery was propping up the bar.

'He ain't here.' She shrugged her bare shoulders. 'Go after him if you have a mind to venture into territory controlled by Crazy Charles. Yessir, I reckon Crazy Charles would have fun with you. Important galoots enrage him more than most, so I have heard. He'd be sure to think up something special for you, Mr Parker, something far more inventive than a roasting.'

'You're lying. Pickle would never venture anywhere near Crazy Charles. Why should he?'

'Because he's a lawman who is not afraid to do his duty.' It was George Green who spoke. Murmurs of assent greeted the words. 'He was never mad in any event. Mike Herman has confessed to forging the judge's signature,' Green continued.

'He's back in charge,' Miz Jezabel declared. 'And any man who goes gunning for a lawman is a wrong-doer, a lawbreaker himself.' She paused. 'Will said to tell you that you would keep. Right now he has more important matters needing his attention. Those poor Russell girls, in case you have forgotten!'

Missouri saw Boss Parker's face darken with fury.

And some of the men began to speak out, saying that no way were any of them taking on Crazy Charles given what had occurred, for that man was a job for the army and that was a fact.

'Give the men a beer, Miz Jezabel.' Parker withdrew a wad of bills with a flourish. He was looking to save face. 'I'll be along by and by. There's a matter I need to attend to. And for your information, Miz Jezabel, Will Pickle can keep!' Which was more than could be said for the instigator of this mess, his one-time partner Mike Herman.

CHAPTER 9

Simon Parker faced Mike Herman across the bank president's mahogany desk. He forced himself to smile. 'I've got someone I want you to meet, Mike. Let's take a ride. I need to get out of this town for a while. Everywhere I turn, folk are driving me crazy singing Will Pickle's praise. He's won them over.'

Herman nodded. 'He's got to be dealt with. He'll ruin everything, and cost us plenty.' He hid his relief. He had expected to be confronted with a man ready to explode with rage but Parker's mood was affable. A sure sign that Parker had hatched a plan.

'One way or another Pickle will get what's coming!' Parker assured him as the two men made their way towards the livery barn. 'Yep,' Parker continued as they rode out of town, 'folk are fickle. It seems good old Will can do no wrong. He's being praised for single-handedly taking off after the Russell girls. Far from being the butt of town jokes he's a hero now.' Parker paused. 'How the hell he got out of that tumbleweed wagon I do not know. In any event he ain't saying and no one is asking!'

'So who is this galoot you want me to meet?' Herman queried, trying to hide his impatience. 'You seem in a good mood!'

Simon Parker shrugged. 'I've always been able to take whatever life throws at me.' He grinned. 'Here we are. You're gonna get your answer. Just be patient a while longer.'

'Sure thing,' Herman agreed as they dismounted. They had ridden to a secluded spot shielded from view by the lay-out of its rock formation.

'See that satchel? Hand it to me, will you?' Parker ordered.

'Sure thing.' Unsuspecting, Herman reached down towards the battered satchel. The blow to the head that felled him caught him completely unawares and he went down like a pole-axed steer.

Parker was an expert when it came to hogtying steers and he soon had Herman bound and helpless. Only then did he give vent to the rage he had bottled up inside.

'You've caused me one hell of a parcel of trouble,' he bellowed. 'Do you hear me? You've made me look a fool. I have political ambitions. One day the territory will need a governor. They could do worse. You've put it all at risk. If I lock horns with a lawman it's going to throw up one heap of mud. Sure, Pickle may not return but I'm not fool enough to count on that. You're a fool and a liability now, Mike.' He paused. 'And I reckon it's time to deal with you.' He picked up the satchel and opened it. He held aloft the gunny sack which emerged. 'Did I ever tell you I grew up in mountain country? Hell, we belonged to some weird kind of religious community. Yep, we danced with snakes to prove our righteousness. And with that kind of upbringing a man knows how to handle a snake. I've one right here. I'm gonna introduce you to this little beauty!'

Herman's terror-filled eyes fixed themselves on the wriggling bag.

'Getting them out of the bag and grabbing them at the neck, now that takes a whole parcel of courage and luck. Yep, every now and then we'd lose a member of the congregation,' Parker continued conversationally. 'Got you.' He held the snake up triumphantly. 'You're gonna die, Mike Herman. You're gonna be bitten on your cheek by a goddamn rattler. I've had a bellyful of you. I am dissolving our partnership!'

Mile Herman began to scream, to beg and finally, when he realized he was done for, to sob with terror.

It felt good jabbing the rattler's head against Herman's cheek. Parker imagined that the victim was Will Pickle, that goddamn thorn in his side. He never would have imagined that the dirt-farmer could have caused him so much trouble. Why, just thinking about the man caused him to seethe with rage. He'd been a fool. He ought to have put a rattler to Will Pickle when they had him helpless. Leaving the man to rot in an asylum had appealed to him more at the time and it had certainly earned Mrs Parker's approval.

With a grunt he hurled the snake away and then settled down to watch Herman die. No one would care what had happened to the bank president and if the man were fool enough to get himself bitten by a rattler he had only himself to blame. As Herman breathed his final breath Parker found himself wondering what Pickle was up to.

'We had one,' the fat man told Will Pickle. He belched. Small eyes peered at Will. He grinned flashing gold teeth before he continued; 'But you are too late, *señor*. She has killed herself. She stabbed herself in the belly.' He laughed. 'But she did not do a good job.' He shook his head, evidencing mock sympathy. 'She took a long time to die.' When Will did not speak the fat man continued persuasively: 'Why not try another one of my girls? They are all superb. I can vouch for them myself. You will not be disappointed.'

The man's callous indifference only served to fuel Will's rage. 'Too bad for you she is dead!' he rejoined coldly.

Unease showed in those small, dark, pebble eyes. 'You knew her?' the fat man questioned questioned uncertainly.

'I know of her,' Will replied. 'You told me!' He could see the louse did not understand his meaning. 'I'm gonna blast you!'

'Why!' the varmint was at a loss to understand.

'Because I can.' Will's voice was flat. 'I'm counting to five. Make your move!'

At the count of three the terrified proprietor reached. So did two of his customers. Will blasted both of them as well. The guns seemed to jump into his hands, aiming and firing with an ease that erroneously suggested he had been killing folk for years.

The acrid smell of gunsmoke hung in the air. He scanned the room, seeking any sign of movement. Three customers sat as if turned to stone. He was about to leave when it occurred to him that he must do his damnedest to discourage the buying of stolen women. Fear was the key.

'You there!' Will pointed at a quaking patron, a ratlike little fellow, who clearly believed he was about to be blasted.

'*Si?*' he quavered.

'Get your knife out real slow,' Will ordered. 'Real slow, do you hear! One wrong move and you are done for. Good. Now cut off their ears and wrap them in your bandanna.' The man obeyed. 'Toss it on to the table.' Carefully Will retrieved the blood-soaked bundle. 'I want men to listen to what I have to say,' he continued. 'And that is there ain't going to be any more stolen women bought and forced to work in this cantina. If I hear tell of any I'm gonna do far worse than take ears off galoots who don't need them. Savvy! Good. Now I'm heading out. Stay put if you want to keep living.' Carefully he backed towards the door. His horse was ready and waiting outside. He had four more places to check out in his quest to find the Russell girls.

Simon Parker relaxed in the barber's chair as Salvo the barber lathered his face. The man was complaining about Miz Gatrell. 'I need a doctor,' Salvo griped. 'I ain't dropping my trousers in front of that woman. It ain't right.'

'Well, she ain't too bad. She knows more about doctoring than her no-account brother ever did.' George Green seemed to be defending the woman. 'Say,' he continued, addressing Salvo, 'I reckon Will Pickle is sweet on Miz Jezabel. What do you say?'

'Yep, I reckon he is,' Salvo agreed. 'Sure as hell she is kindly disposed towards him.'

'I'm here for a shave. Quit gabbing,' the rancher snarled angrily, even here in the barber's shop he was unable to get away from that damn dangerous fool Will Pickle! If he had been a praying man he would have prayed that the crazed renegade would cut Pickle into small pieces real slow. Just hearing the name Pickle filled him with a red rage and made him want to vomit.

Parker paid the barber and left. His mood was foul. A man could not even have a peaceful shave without hearing that darn name. He needed a drink.

Both men fell silent. Neither believed for one minute that Mike Herman had accidentally connected with a rattlesnake. Herman's bloated, blotched face had not been a pretty sight. He was buried now, planted without ceremony. Folk were wondering who was going to take over at the bank but no one was much concerned about Herman's so-called accidental encounter. Folk who had owed money were indeed mighty relieved.

Will Pickle smelt the town before he arrived, a sure sign that their garbage was not being buried but dumped. Dawn was just beginning to break. It was

112

the grey time between the end of night and the beginning of day, a time that had always appealed to Will although it did not suit many. In the old days he would have been up making Gertrude her pot of hot, sweet tea. Now here he was riding into a small Mexican town, bandanna over his nose, trying not to puke at the stench. Why, once the heat of the day struck this festering pile of garbage it would be awash with flies, covered in a thick blanket of the varmints. They always appeared from nowhere when a stench went up. He cursed softly. An object had caught his eye, something, or rather someone, a body had been carelessly dumped amongst the garbage.

Absent mindedly he fingered his badge. He felled compelled to investigate. He was a lawman, after all. The dead man certainly was not a Mexican. He was from across the border, same as Will, and he had died recently, maybe last night by the look of things. Will pulled up the blood-soaked and stiffened heavy plaid shirt to reveal a belly that had been cut wide open; he'd been opened up the way a man might open up a can. It didn't seem right going through the galoot's pocket, but it had to be done. As he had expected he found nothing that might shed light on the killing.

A scuffling sound brought him to his feet, reaching for his Colt .45. Two young 'uns had crept up on him. They stood as if frozen, clearly expecting to be blasted. Will forced a smile. He guessed he knew why they were here. They had come for the dead man's clothes and boots. He could not blame them for that. Times were hard, folk had to make do as best they could. And whoever this man was he had no further need of clothing or boots. Slowly, taking care not to startle them he produced a wad of bills. Two pairs of bright eyes fixed on the bills. He peeled off a few. 'Anyone want to tell me who he is and what he is doing here?' he asked softly, mindful that they might not know in any event or, if they were smart enough they would make up a convincing story. What the hell, they could have a few bills in any event, courtesy of Mike Herman and the bank.

Eager for the money the older of the two boys began to babble. News spread fast in these small place and by the time they had finished Will was pretty sure he had learned the truth. He dropped the bills on to the ground and in excellent Spanish warned the two to forget that they had seen him and not to flash the money around or very likely they themselves would end up lying dead and waiting to be buried under a deluge of garbage. Choice had been taken from his hands. Confrontation could not be avoided. The man from over the border had come here with the same intention as Will. He had wanted to buy back a stolen woman. And they had taken his money, lured him into thinking all would be well before carving him up and throwing him on to the garbage dump.

The owner of the cantina was called Benito and he exercised absolute power over the stolen women forced to work for him. He had been having trouble with the latest arrival.

'I am your master,' he hollered. 'You work for me!

You make me rich.' With that he raised his fist, determined to knock her into compliance. It always worked. 'I want to hear you say it,' he continued, You're gonna tell me that I am your master!'

Will entered the place as dusk was falling. It smelt of wine and cigars. The lamps were low. A few men sat at a table playing cards.

'Women,' he slurred. 'Let me see all you have!' He waved a wad of money. 'It's been a hell of a long time . . .' He swayed on his feet as he advanced into the pit of evil, as Gertrude would have called it.

'Sí, sí!' Benito was eager to oblige. He yelled out to someone to fetch the girls pretty damn quick.

Will grinned foolishly. If he had his way this was gonna be over with pretty damn quick.

'You the owner?'

'*Sí, sí!*' Benito rubbed his hands together. And made the mistake of nodding perceptively. A galoot at the table nodded back. Clearly they thought the stranger too damn drunk to notice. 'Get the women out,' Benito ordered.

He'd have to kill them all. It was a sobering thought. But these galoots had no business in a place that used women stolen from across the border. Also they had just been given the go-ahead to carve up another poor pilgrim. He had to blast them to save his own hide. Damned if he was going to allow himself to be dispatched and dumped on a garbage heap. Hell, if he wound up dead the women would be back where they started. He was their only chance.

No need to justify yourself, Will. He could almost hear the voices of his dead wife and his father-in-law. *Get on with it*, the old man yelled impatiently. Hearing those voices was a sure sign that he was on edge, for killing was not his forte. Hell, how he almost wished he'd never pinned on the star, but in that event he would not have become acquainted with Miz Jezabel.

Pityingly he eyed the poor critters now being paraded before him. There were no Miz Jezabels in this place. None of these women would ever be so bold as to cuss and threaten a customer. No customer would ever back away in fear from one of these shaking, snivelling girls. Nor were the Russell girls here. Darn it, his quest was not yet concluded.

'Is this all of them!' he yelled. 'I don't reckon to any of these. If you have any others get them out.'

'No, no.' Benito shook his head. 'These four are all I have just now, although I may get new ones in a month or so.'

'Well, I won't be here.' He eyed the women. 'Speak up. Are you the only ones? I'll know if you lie.'

'Dottie is upstairs,' a girl quavered.

'Get her down,' Will yelled. 'My money is as good as anyone's. Ain't that right? Ain't that right?' he rounded on Benito.

Benito smiled ingratiatingly. 'Of course *señor.*' Let him take his pleasure first, he thought, then they would carve him up as he left. 'You are the boss,' he soothed.

Will could see why they had kept the fifth woman out of view. Her face was bruised and battered – and the rest of her too, he surmised from the way she moved.

'That's it then?' he queried.

'*Sí.*' Benito nodded, the last thing he ever did, for Will without warning hauled iron. The women screamed as the men went down, blood seeping on to the scuffed floorboards as they died.

'Shut up,' Will yelled, trying to shut his ears to their scream's. 'I am a lawman. Here to save you. I'm taking you home. I have two more to collect and then we're all heading back across the Rio Grande. Now pull yourselves together, grab a blanket each, for the nights are cold. Get moving. We're heading out pronto.' These women were a chain around his neck but what could he do but play the cards as they were dealt?

To his surprise the one called Dottie, the one who had been beaten, had taken charge of the other four. 'Get them damn blankets,' Dottie screamed as she discarded her useless fancy shoes that she'd been forced to wear. 'And extra blankets. Get. We're going home. Ain't that right, Mister?'

'We sure are.' Will took the opportunity to help himself to a few more ears. Word was going to spread in these border towns. Men would be reluctant now to buy from Crazy Charles.

Simon Parker was now drunk. He rested his elbows on the bar of the Naked Lady saloon as he watched Miz Jezabel good-naturedly turning down a customer who had asked to become better acquainted.

'Now Bert, this is my place and I don't choose to go upstairs.'

'Not even if I change my name to Pickle!' Bert cackled.

Miz Jezabel pinched his ear and with a laugh warned him to mind his manners. 'Sure thing, Miz Jezabel, sure thing,' the fool rejoined. 'I ain't of a mind to step on Will's toes.'

'Well, I am glad to hear it, Bert. But you may buy me a beer,' she replied with a wink.

'Sure thing, Miz Jezabel!'

That uppity woman riled him plenty. She did not know her place. And no one in this goddamn town was man enough to put her in that place. He decided she needed a real man to show her what was what. He lurched towards her.

'I aim to find out what Pickle finds attractive in you, Miz Jezabel.' He eyed her up and down insultingly. 'What it can be I can't say, for you are mighty long in the tooth, Miz Jezabel, but I guess Will Pickle ain't particular.'

Miz Jezabel turned away. This insult could not be allowed. If he got away with it others would be tempted to step out of line. It was not her way to turn the other cheek.

'I'm gonna show you just what Will Pickle finds so attractive,' she promised as she reached for the hem of a red skirt.

'I can't wait, Miz Jezabel, I can't wait.' Simon Parker hooted with laughter.

'And neither can I,' she screeched. As she spun round the knife which had emerged from beneath her skirt buried itself in his stomach, sinking in to the hilt with the force of the thrust. 'There ain't no one insults me without paying the price,' she screamed. 'Long in the tooth am I? Well maybe I am but I can handle the likes of you, Simon Parker and any other galoot who steps over the line.'

Simon Parker lay dying on the sawdust scattered floor of the Naked Lady saloon. He had not seen it coming, never anticipated she would commit such an outrageous act, never realized how she would react to his insults. Blood pooled beneath him. He tried to speak. His eyes closed and then he was gone.

'Well he's done for, Miz Jezabel, or soon will be,' Bert essayed. He scratched his head. 'Well, I had best walk you over to Miz Gatrell just in case you take a turn.'

'Take a turn, Bert?' She looked at him without comprehension.

'It's what women do, Miz Jezabel,' Bert persisted. He paused. 'Sure as hell Will Pickle would walk you over to see Miz Gatretll and I can do no less.'

Without a downward glance she stepped over the body of Simon Parker.

'Of course, if you were a man, Miz Jezabel, you could have called him out,' Bert soothed. 'Lord, I hope Will gets back real soon. He'll see things your way, Miz Jezabel no doubt about it but—'

'Quit gabbing Bert. I'll go along with you walking me over to Miz Gatrell but I don't want to hear another word about this matter.'

'Yes ma'am,' he muttered. Sure as hell Will Pickle had best return soon for there would be Mrs Dora Parker to deal with. And that woman would not let the matter rest until she'd been avenged.

*

The newly widowed Mrs Dora Parker shut herself in the bedroom. She screamed and cursed and smashed a wall mirror to pieces, cutting herself in the process. She kept on screaming until her throat was hoarse and then she sat down at her writing-desk. She was the boss now. The men would follow her orders. The first task, the most important task of all, was to pen a missive for Sheriff Walt Lock. A man would be dispatched with that missive. That vile creature calling herself Miz Jezabel was going to hang for this. Too bad the hanging judge could not be called upon to pronounce sentence but he was dead, so she had heard, found with his neck snapped in an alleyway. But she was sure Walt Lock, when apprised of this outrage, could manage very well without the presence of a judge.

Why, the woman could be brought here and hanged from the tree that grew opposite her front porch. She could sit on her porch and watch the proceedings from her old rocking-chair as the creature choked and struggled to live. The thought comforted her. She did not doubt that Walt Lock would come. He was a committed lawman after all, which was more that could be said for the disgraceful Will Pickle.

Will scratched his chin; one of them had realized that by cutting a hole in a blanket it could be worn as a cape. They were all covered now, more or less, which was just as well as the night was becoming chill. He did not know whether anyone would come after them. He risked a fire and brewed coffee, cooking up a coarse oatmeal porridge which one of them took him to task for, telling him that his coffee and porridge were no damn good. He was glad to see none of them seemed to be going mad. No one had 'taken a turn' as it was often referred to. And two of them were arguing that he ought to forget about the Russell girls, for now at least, as they all needed to get back across the border pretty damn quick. But he stood firm, closing his ears until eventually they let him be, one by one falling into troubled sleep. He was in one hell of a predicament and he knew it.

CHAPTER 10

'What's this all about?' Walt Lock grunted impatiently. The missive ran into six pages, the hand writing was small and cramped. He could scarcely be bothered to read it.

'Miz Jezabel, proprietor of the Naked Lady saloon, has done for Simon Parker,' the waddy explained. 'Yep, he riled her plenty and she knifed him. Miz Parker wants Miz Jezabel hung from the tree in front of her porch. Sheriff Pickle won't do it. He's away in Mexico. Besides which he is sweet on Miz Jezabel.'

'Pickle? I thought he was headed for an asylum! What happened to Sheriff Worth?'

'Bradley Worth is dead, killed by renegades.' The waddy paused. 'And as for Pickle, seems it was all a mistake, so they say.'

Walt Lock shrugged. He did not give a damn either way. 'So what do you think of all this. Do you want to see Miz Jezabel hung?'

'Me! Hell, Miz Parker pays my wages. She said deliver this missive and that's what I've done. I'm headed for the saloon. I sure have a powerful thirst.'

The waddy did not much care for Sheriff Lock.

Walt Lock studied the missive, which had clearly been written in haste by the bereaved Miz Parker. He could never admit it, but he had developed a taste for hanging. He liked to watch men and women kicking at the end of a rope. But he could not be seen to be too eager to involve himself in this matter. He yelled out for his right-hand man Jack Jackson to get his butt into the office. Succinctly Walt explained the situation, adding: 'I'm gonna toss a coin, Jack. Heads we go. Tails we stay. You tell me how it falls.' He tossed the coin.

'Heads,' Jackson announced sourly. 'Hell, Walt, we've just got back from Galbraith!'

'Inconvenience goes with the job,' Walt rejoined. He lit a match and set fire to the missive. He liked watching how the flames ate away at the paper. 'And a respectable ranching man has been killed, knifed by a no-account saloon woman. I feel obliged to do my duty.'

'You're gonna have trouble rustling up a posse,' Jackson observed. 'This matter ain't one of pressing urgency and the men are damn tired.'

'That's as maybe. But men who pin on a badge ain't allowed the luxury of feeling damn tired.'

'Hell, I reckon it's gonna be just you and me then!' Jackson griped.

Walt laughed 'Maybe, but we can handle that damn female solo. We don't need back-up.'

'I'm obliged to do my duty,' Will Pickle declared. Dissension had broken out amongst the rescued women. Some of them were saying he must forget about the Russell girls and get the rest of them safely back across the border. They had reached the little town of Santa Maria, where Will was hoping to find the two girls. He sighed. 'Well, I have done my damnedest. If they ain't here I will get you ladies safely back and then resume my search.'

'You're like a dog with a bone,' Dottie declared. 'You won't give it up! And your persistence will likely be the death of you!'

Will ignored the remark. 'Just keep the girls hidden and quiet,' he ordered. 'I'll be as quick as I can.' He was all too aware that the killing was getting easier now. It was done without thought, the way a man might swat a fly, the dead being no more to him than flies that had needed to be disposed of.

Gonzales and his cousin had been enjoying the hospitality of Ernesto's cantina when the drunken bum walked in, yelling that he wanted to see all the women and that he aimed to choose the prettiest. He waved a wad of notes by way of incentive. Ernesto, his eyes calculating how much was in the bundle, was keen to oblige, yelling out that they all must show themselves pretty damn quick.

The stranger turned and looked at Gonzales and his cousin. 'Maybe you gents can recommend one,' he slurred, dropping a note on the table.

Gonzales was about to decline but his cousin, who had been drinking steadily from mid afternoon, suddenly belched and declared they would be happy to oblige.

Will nodded. Just as he thought these two varmints didn't deserve to keep breathing.

'Mr Pickle!' A voice quavered and Will found himself face to face with Clara Russell, his neighbour's daughter. Her sister was there also but he could not recall the name of the younger girl.

'She's know you!' Ernesto reached for his shotgun but he was too slow. Will blasted him before it had cleared the top of the bar and then, for good measure, he turned his guns upon the two satisfied customers who, luckily for him as they were drunk, had been slow to react. They fell like sitting ducks.

'I'm here to take you back to Galbraith.' Neither one had a home to go back to now with their ma and pa dead. He hesitated, unwilling to help himself to ears in front of the terrified girls. 'We'll burn this place,' he concluded.

'He's got to pay,' Clara screamed and Will knew she was referring to the renegade. 'You've got to go after him, Mr Pickle. You must.'

Will shook his head. 'Oh, I don't need to look for him. Old Crazy Charles will come looking for me and that is a fact.'

When it suited him Crazy Charles could play the gentleman he had once been. Before he had earned the sobriquet of Crazy Charles his name had been Charles Granley. He came from a wealthy and privileged background and had always known he was far better than other folk.

He was enjoying himself hugely toying with the

young priest, one Father James, late of Ireland, if Charles was not mistaken. He had no time for priests, one had denounced him as a murderer thus necessitating his removal from civilization for the savagery of the frontier. Poor Father James thought his black robe and stiff white collar were going to save him.

'I have always been a religious man,' Charles had said, much to the amazement of his men who had expected him to kill the priest without further ado. 'Let's discuss this matter over a glass of wine.' Charles had paused. 'Quite a lot of what they say about me is a fabrication of the truth.'

So poor Father James, nodding his too large head, had agreed to take a glass of wine with the monster.

'I deny that I have ever cut the heart out of anyone and ate it,' Charles remarked conversationally, enjoying the way Father James's face blanched. 'It's a downright lie and that's a fact. Moreover it is a heathen practice and I am no heathen. I am a gentleman.'

'Quite so,' Father James agreed as he forced a ghastly smile at this for now, he hoped, benign monster.

'I admire your courage,' Charles continued, knowing full well that Father James was quaking in his boots. 'I cannot think of one man who would dare defy me, not one!'

His voice oozed satisfaction. 'Such is the power of fear,' he continued. 'Now, are you prepared to hand that runaway woman over? She had no business bolting.' He shook his head. 'We aren't going to kill her, just teach her a lesson and return her to her place of work. Hand Esmeralda over and you will hear no more from me.' And he meant it. Father James, being an honourable man, would be driven mad by his own conscience and that would be torment enough for one like him.

To his shame Father James was tempted. But the moment passed. 'No,' he said quietly. 'And if you have any regard for your immortal soul you will leave us in peace.'

'Well, I ain't!' The gentleman was gone, he snapped his fingers. 'I want you to know what worthless bums you have been ministering to, snivelling yellow-bellied cowards the lot of them. I want you to know you are a damn fool. I'm going to give you plenty of time to pray for my immortal soul and your own.' He paused. 'Pedro, string this varmint up by his heels and leave him hanging from that tree yonder. He's going to hang there till he rots and not one of these varmints is going to cut him down for fear of displeasing me. Anyone who displeases me is gonna be chopped into pieces little by little. Get on with it!'

Esmeralda, watching from the bell-tower of the church, saw them drag Father James into the middle of the little square. Crying, she watched as they strung him from the tree.

Crazy Charles directed his gaze at the bell-tower. He shook his fists. 'Now for you, missy, now for you,' he yelled. 'Go get her!' Howling like mad dogs his men rushed towards the bell-tower.

Esmeralda stifled a sob. And did the only thing left to do. Uttering a piercing scream she jumped from the top of the tower, hitting the ground with a sickening thud and dying instantly.

'Damnation!' a man yelled. 'She's cheated us!'

Crazy Charles shrugged. 'That's women for you! We will rest here awhile. You men root around and see if you can dig out anything that takes your fancy. See that Father James watches you enjoying yourself. I'm heading up into the bell-tower. Some one needs to keep a look-out for signs of trouble. And make sure Esmeralda remains where she has fallen. The buzzards are welcome to her.'

When Gonzales rode into town night was falling. A bonfire had been lit before the church and drunken men lounged around the bonfire, amusing them-selves with screaming women, the priest, still squirm-ing, hung from a tree. Crazy Charles, unless Gonzales were mistaken, would be found in the bell-tower. Gonzales knew the crazy galoot liked to get as close to the sky as he could this being one of Charles's idio-syncrasies.

Gasping, Gonzales climbed the seemingly never-ending steps of the bell-tower. 'Well, he is here!' Gonzales announced without preamble when he reached his boss.

'What the hell are you talking about?'

'The one galoot who ain't troubled about riling you. He's taken them back, the women you sold. And the men he's killed, why, he is collecting their ears. Ernesto's place has been burned to the ground. He's a lawman, it seems, for he is wearing a star.' Gonzales expected Charles to go berserk but the man remained calm.

Walt Lock don't give a hoot about stolen women as long as they ain't from his territory, Charles mused. It could not be Walt Lock. And that only left a lawman out of the town of Galbraith. The two-bit town had already lost a lawman and a posse. Surely no one was fool enough to come after him. But it seemed someone was, a lone rider who had wreaked havoc, a crazy bastard who didn't give a damn by the sound of him.

Charles headed for the steps that led down from the bell-tower. That crazy varmint would regret the day he'd poked his nose into matters that were not his concern. There was no time to be lost; the women had to be sent packing and the drunken bums he controlled must be forced to sober up pretty damn quick, for they had to ride at break of day. They'd head for the point in the river that was the nearest crossing-place for the town of Galbraith. With luck he could get the damn lawman before he crossed back. And he must dispatch two men to Galbraith, just in case the varmint was already across the river. There would be no safety in Galbraith. This man had thrown down the gauntlet and Charles aimed to pick it up. Dealing with this crazy galoot gave him something to look forward to!

If he were honest Will had to admit he would be glad to be free of the burden these women presented. They were a damn weight on his shoulders and getting heavier by the day with their nightmares and sobbing. Thank the Lord Dottie had taken charge, marshalling them along and keeping them moving as they headed towards safety.

He had decided to give Galbraith a wide berth. The renegade would look for them there. Crazy Charles could not let things be. He had lost face. He survived because the folk he terrorized thought him invincible. Once he lost face the balance would be altered. Yep, if needs be Charles would follow Will to hell and back. Women sold by Crazy Charles could not be allowed to regain their freedom.

'It's Fort Beacon,' Will had told the protesting females. 'And no arguing about it. I reckon you'll be safe inside an army fort, far safer than in Galbraith as matters stand at the moment.'

'Goddamnit, Will Pickle, you are taking us out of our way,' Dottie had cried in exasperation. 'The longer it takes to reach civilization the better chance he has of finding us.'

'Maybe so. But he's got to learn about us before he starts looking, and I am gambling that we can make it safely to Fort Beacon.'

'You obstinate mule, you are gambling with our lives.'

'Well, I can't help that. I'm making the decisions. Yell all you like, Miss Dottie, it will not change a damn thing!' With that he had led the protesting women in the direction of Fort Beacon.

It had been a hell of a trek. But it seemed the gamble had paid off. The river lay before them, a silver twisting ribbon cutting the harsh landscape in half. It was then that he saw them; two travellers likewise making for the river. 'Wait here.' He urged his horse forward ready for trouble, although the two looked harmless enough.

'Howdy there,' he remarked pleasantly as he regarded the pair, an old woman riding a *burro* and the young boy walking beside her. The *burro* was loaded down with water-bags and a woven basket that contained squawking chickens.

'Where'd you get those girls,' the old woman asked.

'I've rescued them. We're heading for Fort Beacon.' He saw no reason to hide the truth.

'Me too,' she replied. 'Can you spare a few coins?'

'Sure.' Will handed them to the boy, who wasn't a boy at all but a girl dressed as one.

'Well, it seems you missed Esmeralda.' She pocketed the coins. 'She came home. I left before Crazy Charles arrived. It's safer that way. Poor Father James, he's dead meat.'

'Where are you from?' Will asked hoarsely. Goddamnit, the was acquainted with Father James; the young man had stopped by the farm on his way to Mexico.

'Why do you want to know?'

'Because I've got to go there.' He could not cross the river now. He could not continue to Fort Beacon. Raising his arm he beckoned for the women to ride on down. 'You know how to get to Fort Beacon?' he queried. She stuck a pipe between toothless gums and he realized that that was a darn fool question. 'I'll pay you to guide these girls to Fort Beacon, see them safe.'

She held out a gnarled hand, rapidly pocketing the notes that Will thrust into her palm. 'You play me false and your granddaughter ain't going to see

131

another birthday,' he threatened, then immediately felt ashamed of himself. To his relief she ignored him and headed her *burro* towards the river.

'What the hell are you up to now?' Dottie demanded.

'I've got to go back. I've got to visit Santa Rosa. A good man needs me. And I have a hunch you women will be safe enough. That varmint ain't yet on our trail. It seems he has been attending to other matters. Lady Luck has favoured us!'

'Lady Luck!' she screamed. 'Don't you dare talk about Lady Luck after the way we have all suffered! You're a dead man if you go back. You know that!'

'No I don't. Besides which the late Mrs Pickle liked to read the cards and she assured me one time that I was destined for long life.' And it was true, not that he had believed a word of it. 'Now get along. Your new guide ain't waiting for you. Just stick close. She may be old but she had sense enough to get her granddaughter out of Santa Rosa before old Crazy Charles arrived in town. He paused. 'When you arrive at Fort Beacon there's no reason to keep my whereabouts a secret. Spread the word if you like. I've a hunch I'm destined to meet old Crazy Charles real soon.

'I'm coming with you, Mr Pickle,' Clara Russell spoke up defiantly.

'No you ain't.' This was all he needed.

'Yes I am. I saw what that varmint did to my ma. I've got the right.'

'Well, I reckon you have, but if I think Crazy Charles is going to get his hands on you I will feel obliged to blast you first,' he warned, hoping to deter her.

'Fair enough.' To his amazement she held out her hand, which he felt obliged to shake. Frontier life was hard. And those who could not survive it soon went under. He guessed all these women would survive their ordeal. Leastways, he hoped so but a man could never tell. 'We ain't riding into Santa Rosa guns blazing,' he advised. 'We're sneaking in late at night without drawing attention to ourselves. What I aim to do I don't know. I guess I will work that out along the way, depending upon how the cards fall.'

Ramrod Sid Lowe frowned when he saw old Moses riding in. 'There ain't no job for you here,' he told the oldster bluntly. 'Fact is, you can't pull your weight.'

The old man cackled. 'Oh, I ain't looking for work. Why, I am here to help out Miz Parker in her hour of need. I'll clean out the stables in return for one good meal a day. What do you say. Boss Parker was mighty good to me. I aim to repay him best way I can.'

'The man's dead!' Sid stated bluntly. 'And the fool brought it upon himself, baiting that she devil Miz Jezabel.'

'But he's looking down on us, ain't he?' Moses declared. 'So the Good Book says.'

'Well, do what you like. We can't pay you but I reckon we can feed you. Miz Parker won't even notice you. She's inside being fussed over by two or three women from town. She's taken poorly and claiming she can scarce stand.'

'Thank you kindly, Sid,' old Moses cackled. 'She'll be fine by and by,' he added with another cackle.

'Yep, when she sees Miz Jezabel dangling,' Sid rejoined. There was a lengthy silence. Sid was not a man to kick an old dog and Moses reminded him of an old dog. 'Say, you were darn lucky Pickle didn't blast you,' he essayed, but the old coot wasn't listening. He guessed he knew why the old man was here. It stood to reason Pickle would not be coming back. And it figured that sooner or later Pickle's replacement would boot old Moses out of the jailhouse.

Moses headed into the barn. Of late he had been feeling poorly. Pains across his chest were delivering the message that maybe his time had run out. He prayed he could hang on a mite longer. He aimed to repay Will Pickle the only way he knew. Lord, that man had no business crossing the border. He ought to have stayed around to watch out for Miz Jezabel.

CHAPTER 11

Miz Jezabel lit a cigar. She realized she was in big trouble. There were mutterings in town to the effect that Simon Parker had been murdered. Some were saying it was a disgrace that the killer still walked free. Poor Simon Parker had not stood a chance, they said. How could he have known what she was going to do? Worse than that, Mrs Dora Parker had sent for Sheriff Walt Lock and that man really was trouble! Naturally there was no sign of Will Pickle when she needed him!

Regrettably, she had decided that she had best leave town. She was not exactly worried about Walt Lock, she told herself, but hell, she would feel happier if Will Pickle were around. As she wanted to keep on breathing, there was no choice. She had to fork it out pretty damn quick. Why, she had delayed too long already and all on account of that obstinate mule Will Pickle. She had wasted time waiting for him to return. The stage was due pretty soon, and she must resign herself to the fact that she had seen the last of him.

Will Pickle let rip with a string of profanities. The dangling remains of poor Father James were not a pleasant sight. Clara Russell, turning away, was physically sick. She ought not to be here. She was a burden, not a help, but there had been a wild glint in her eye when she had insisted on accompanying him. So he had backed down and regretted it ever since.

Will drew his blade and cut Father James down.

'Goddamnit,' he yelled, unable to contain his rage. 'You miserable bastards. Anyone of you could have cut him down and saved his life. You've failed him, the whole damn lot of you. Yellow-bellies the whole damn bunch of you!'

The street was empty. They were all cowering indoors, even though Crazy Charles had been long gone. They had all been too petrified to help their priest, such was the terror the renegade could arouse even from afar.

'Shall we bury him?' Clara Russell sobbed.

'Nope,' Will rejoined grimly, 'I have thought of a more fitting kind of send-off, one more in keeping with what has occurred.' He did not elaborate but tied a bandanna over his nostrils. He must carry these pitiful remains inside the church. The remains of poor unfortunate Esmeralda must also be set to rest inside the church. 'You varmints ain't fit to lick this brave man's boots,' he bellowed as he carried what was left of Father James into the church.

There was no reply. He knew they would all remain cowering inside thick walls until the showdown was over. They all knew Crazy Charles would be back once word reached him that the man he wanted was within his grasp.

Moses was finding it harder to stir himself in the mornings. But he managed to keep going, greeting men around the ranch with a cheerful cackle as he enthusiastically cleaned out the stables, a chore none of them wanted to do. Why, they scarcely noticed his presence. And that was just the way he wanted it. He aimed to stay alive until he had repaid Sheriff Pickle.

When the waddy from town arrived the youngster likewise didn't give the oldster a glance.

'Things sure are moving,' he yelled out, as men eager for news surrounded him. 'Sheriff Walt Lock has arrived in Galbraith,' he informed everyone. 'But Miz Jezabel has hoofed it out.'

'Hoofed!' a man queried.

'She's taken the stage.'

'Then why the hell didn't you say so?'

'And Lock has been prevailed upon to go after her,' the waddy continued. 'The town council had a word, so it seemed, and persuaded him it was his duty to bring her to justice. And they offered him a cash inducement to boot, so keen are they to get her back.'

'Damn bastards,' Moses muttered. No one paid him any attention. They were used to the old man muttering to himself.

'What about Pickle?' a waddy asked.

'No word as yet.' Young Morgan, the messenger,

paused. Clearly he enjoyed being the object of attention. 'But,' he continued slowly, 'the stolen women have turned up at Fort Beacon. He's rescued about seven of them, so they say. It seems Pickle has been on a killing spree across the border. Word is he is still in Mexico attending to unfinished business.'

'Why, the man is a damn fool!'

'More than that, he's crazy,' someone observed.

'He'll be crazier still when he finds Miz Jezabel has been hung!'

'But it will be Walt Lock he'll go after,' Sid Lowe pointed out. 'Assuming he ever gets back from Mexico. Hell, I would not want to be in his shoes. Crazy Charles is one mean-hearted varmint!'

'I can be a mean-hearted varmint myself,' Moses cackled. 'And that's a fact.' Things were beginning to come together. And he aimed to quit this life with a bang! Why the hell did younger folk think men became affable when they got old? Hell, now I've got them all thinking I have turned into an affable old fool, he thought. That was not the way he aimed to be remembered. And sure as hell he was going to repay the debt he owed Sheriff Pickle. Leaning on his shovel he watched as the young waddy headed for the ranch house, and Mrs Dora Parker. Much to Moses' disgust three chairs had already been set on the veranda in anticipation of the hanging of Miz Jezabel.

'Get back to town,' Mrs Parker ordered, dramatically revived by the news that Sheriff Lock was in pursuit of Miz Jezabel. 'You get back to town and remind folk that I want her brought here. I have the

right to see her hang for she has made me a widow.'
Mrs Parker determined to take a little chicken soup.
She needed her strength for what was to come.
Justice had to be done and she was obliged to witness
it.

Since cutting down Father James Will had done his
damnedest to convince folk that he was loco. The
crazier they all thought him the better. His plan
hinged on their thinking him crazy.

As he was not crazy he soon enough spotted the
stinking fish when he saw it. The galoot who had
gone running to Crazy Charles when Esmeralda had
sought sanctuary in the church! The stinking fish
answered to the name of Santino. He was young. He
was handsome. His teeth flashed white and he had
made an impression on Clara. Young Santino had
emerged from behind the thick, white, stone walls of
his home; he had come out fishing for information,
pathetically eager to know for how long they planned
to stay in town.

'He can't be blamed for being afraid.' Clara
defended Santino. 'To have cut poor Father James
down would have been to invite a terrible death.'

'Yep, maybe so but you would have done it and so
would I,' Will had agreed. He found he had no time
for cowardly bums. And Lord knew this little town
was full of them. She had a lot to learn. 'Doesn't it
occur to you that young Santino is asking a mite too
many questions?'

'I just told him what you said to tell him,' she
replied.

Will sighed. Sure as hell he wished the late Mrs Pickle were here or Miz Jezabel. It did not set right having to rely on young Clara Russell to see matters through. She could go to pieces at any time.

'Well, I am sorry to tell you Miss Clara, that even as we speak young Santino is on his way to betray us. He aims to come back with Crazy Charles. He might have liked your smile Miss Clara, but I reckon he likes the glint of a coin far better. Now you had best get up to the bell-tower and keep watch. Events are going to start moving from now on. Old Crazy Charles will be coming to town and this time he's going to be dealt with just as he deserves.'

'Are you intending to propose to Miz Jezabel?'

'Just you get up to the bell-tower. I'll attend to other matters. Remember that we have got to be prepared and ready every moment from now on until it is over with. Miss Clara, I am counting on you. If you don't do this right we are both done for and that's a fact.'

Miz Jezabel lit another cigar. Fate was conspiring against her. A wheel had come off the goddamn coach. Fortunately the coach was not moving at the time. The wheel had come loose as they had pulled into the stage depot.

Hughie, the stage driver, scratched his head. 'We're gonna be here awhile,' he advised. 'Stretch your legs. Once we're moving we're gonna fly like the devil himself is after us!' He laughed, unaware that as far as Miz Jezabel was concerned, very likely the devil in the form of Walt Lock was on her heels.

'It can't be rushed,' he advised the travelling sales-man who had presumed to tell him to get on with it. 'Now let me be,' Hughie advised.

Miz Jezabel wandered around. Then, as it became clear they must spend a second night at the stop-over, sauntered back inside. Her three fellow-passengers, the salesman and two lone females, were shunning her. Disapproving looks were directed every time she lit up a cigar. Being on edge she was lighting up more than was normal. Out of sight, out of mind so they said. She knew it wasn't true. She kept thinking about Will Pickle. She was also thinking about Walt Lock.

Crazy Charles lit a cigar. So, the man they sought was in Santa Rosa, spending his time preaching to an empty church.

'He is loco,' Santino continued. 'It must be so. He stays in the church with the rotting remains of Father James and Esmeralda. The smell is so strong now and there are flies also. Sometimes he preaches from the pulpit with only the girl to hear him. She cannot leave. There is no one to help her except the mad man. She tells me he says he is about the Lord's work. Yes, he is truly crazy.'

Crazy Charles nodded. He had seen men who had been driven mad. Indeed he had deliberately driven a good many of them mad all by himself. He felt a moment's disappointment that the man, Will Pickle, had already gone mad. He would have liked to drive Will Pickle mad little by little. He began to imagine how he would torture this enemy. The runaway girl scarcely mattered. It was the lawman he wanted.

'I have done well?' Santino sought approval.

'You sure as hell have and you are gonna do better. Before I make my move you are going to ride into town, look up Will Pickle and report back what he is doing. Knowing one's enemy is the key. I am going to make a special example of this man. He'll be a long time dying, I can tell you. Do you reckon you have the stomach to watch?' He threw the question casually at Santino.

'*Sí, sí,*' Santino agreed quickly.

Crazy Charles nodded. The little squirt would be invited to ride with them; if he refused he would be killed and if he looked away whilst Pickle was being tortured he would likewise be killed. Charles could not abide weakness.

He stood up. 'Let's ride!'

'He's coming.' Clara Russell descended from the bell-tower two steps at a time. 'Santino has returned and he is alone,' she explained. The stench inside the church was overpowering. Her stomach churned. She could scarcely bear to look at the decaying remains of the priest.

Will nodded. The idea had come to him when he had cut Father James down from the tree. There didn't need to be a shoot-out; words did not need to be exchanged and, as the late Mrs Pickle had said, it was possible to get to where one was going by taking more than one path. More than one path led to the point in time when old Crazy Charles faced annihilation.

Will entered the pulpit and started preaching. He was not lost for words. For twenty years he had

142

attended church service with Mrs Pickle. He had been forced to listen to thousands of sermons. Very often they sent him to sleep but not before he had got the gist of what was being said. After today was over he never wanted to listen to another sermon. Wild horses would not get him into a church. Certain memories needed to be buried and what was going to happen today was going to be one of those memories.

Santino entered the church. All was as he had expected. The crazy man was preaching and the girl was crying.

'Stay,' Will cried. 'Stay and listen.'

'Another time, *señor*.' Santino backed from the church, mounted his horse and forked it out to report to Crazy Charles.

Clara Russell began to cry for real. She had liked Santino. 'Leave the bawling until this is over,' Will Pickle advised. 'And just you remember, if you let me down, if we both die here today, there ain't no one going to be around to look after your sister.'

Clara Russell stopped crying. 'When we are done here you may escort me to Fort Beacon. I am going to take my sister to Iowa. We have kin there, folk who will take us in.' She paused. 'What are you going to do, Mr Pickle?'

'Why, guess I will propose to Miz Jezabel,' he rejoined. 'Now get ready, Clara. We can get through this. All we need to do is keep our heads.'

'We've got her!' Walt Lock announced with satisfaction. The two men approached the stage depot on foot, guns drawn and ready to shoot.

'Well, I reckon it would be easier if we were to just blast her. We could say we thought she was reaching for a weapon,' Jack Jackson advised.

Walt glared at his deputy. 'We're lawmen.' It would have been easier but Walt was anticipating the pleasure he would feel watching her choke at the end of a rope. These sentiments could never be admitted. 'No Jack, it won't do. We might not like it but this has got to be done legal. I ain't going to let Mrs Dora Parker down. She is depending on me for justice.'

'I've just got a bad feeling about this. Word is Pickle will come gunning for us after the event. If he makes it back from Mexico.'

'Well then, we must deal with Pickle as we would any other wrongdoer. Clearly the man has lost his senses. There can be no other explanation. Now are you ready?'

Deputy Jackson spat out his plug of chewing baccy. 'Yep.'

There was silence at the table. The boss of the stage depot had tried to sit Miz Jezabel at a side table, away from the so-called respectable folk. She wasn't having any of it. 'If you want to keep on breathing, you had best reconsider,' she advised.

'You sure had,' Hughie interrupted. 'Why, she has already done for rancher Simon Parker. Not that he did not deserve it!' He had winked suggestively. 'Don't you fret, Miz Jezabel, Sheriff Pickle will sort things out.'

It was then that the door exploded inwards. Before Miz Jezabel could react she found herself looking into the mouth of a Colt .45.

'You're going to hang, Miz Jezabel. You're going to face justice. And if you are thinking Will Pickle is going to save you, forget it.' Lock paused. She was looking at him with an expression hard to fathom. 'Get the cuffs on her,' he ordered. And then he could not resist a final jibe, 'Why, I reckon Will Pickle ought to thank me for hanging you, Miz Jezabel. What kind of man wants a woman who sticks a knife into a respectable man's belly just on account of losing her temper. You think of that, Miz Jezabel. Even that dumb galoot cannot be that crazy.'

CHAPTER 12

The church door was partly open, as Santino had said it would be. Even outside the stench emanating from inside the church was overpowering, proof enough that the man was truly loco. Charles noticed that the rope they had used to string up Father James still remained dangling from the branch.

'We could burn him out,' Gonzales suggested boldly, momentarily forgetting that all suggestions came from Crazy Charles.

'We could but we're not going to. Now shut your goddamn mouth. I give the orders around here.'

'Sorry boss.' Gonzales knew he had overstepped the line.

'I want him alive,' Charles continued pleasantly. He grinned. 'Just looking at you, Gonzales, has given me a great idea.'

'Me!' Gonzales swallowed.

'Don't worry your head about it.' Charles had recalled that Gonzales had boasted about being a mighty fine carpenter. So why not have Gonzales build one of these racks used in days gone by.

146

Naturally enough the fool would have to have it all spelled out in minute detail. But Charlie was sure Gonzales could manage it. If not, well, he'd get rid of Gonzales. He just could not abide liars and if Gonzales were not the carpenter he claimed he used to be Gonzales would be in hot water, practically speaking.

'I can't abide liars,' Charles declared.

No one spoke. With good reason! Charles was at his worst when he was grinning that affable, friendly grin which had lulled many into a feeling of false security.

'What the hell!' Gonzales drew his pistol but did not shoot the small boy who now emerged from the church.

'An enterprising young man!' Charles continued to smile. The blockheads he rode with did not understand. Charles pointed at the basket the child carried, filled to the brim with church candles; even the stubs had been taken. 'He's been thieving.' The grin broadened. 'Say, kid, is that crazy galoot still inside?'

The kid nodded vigorously.

'Why the hell didn't he blast you? What did he say?'

'Just said to get the hell out of it and that the Lord was gonna punish me.'

Charles laughed. 'Well, let me tell you, that man is a fool and a damn liar. Now get along home.' He paused. 'If you've a mind you can watch the fun when it starts.'

The kid nodded and then bolted.

147

'He kind of reminds me of myself,' Charles mused, 'Not that I ever had to steal candles.' He forgot about the kid. 'Seems what you say is true, Santino.' He dismounted. 'We're going in. I want him alive. I don't give a damn about the girl. You can do what you like with her. But first let's see how this crazy galoot jumps!' Charles lit a firecracker and tossed it into the doorway of the church.

When the kid had sneaked in with his basket Will had forced himself to maintain the facade of being crazy. He had yelled at the little varmint who, ignoring the yelling, had set about helping himself to the candle-sticks and chalice, placing them carefully into the basket before covering them over with candlesticks. Only when the basket was full had the child headed for the door.

Will had expected to hear the sound of shots. He had expected the renegade to shoot the child. And maybe Charles would have done just that except for the fact that the kid had obviously been stealing. But who knew? With a man such as Charles speculation was futile. Will knew that he was taking the biggest gamble of his life and if he lost both he and Clara were dead.

When the firecracker came through the door he kept right on talking, raising his voice as he recited the Ten Commandments, determined to keep up the pretence to the last.

'Well, he ain't jumping,' Charles had satisfied himself on that score. He could hear the raised voice now, he could make out the words: *thou shalt not kill* being repeated endlessly.

'Let's get this lunatic.' Charles gestured for his men to enter the church. He himself brought up the rear just in case loco Will Pickle started taking random shots. But he did not believe the man was in any condition to make a fight of it. The man had cracked. He had seen this before. He felt a moment's regret that a formidable opponent had changed into this shambling wreck. Killing Pickle would be too damn easy and Charles felt cheated.

Beyond the church door the day was bright. Inside the gloom seemed intensified in contrast to the light. Where the crazy preacher was, he could not say. Evidently the man had scrambled down from the pulpit a moment or so ago. There were plenty of nooks and crannies in this oversized place of worship, with its ornate statues and pillars where a man could hide, at least temporarily.

They were tense, crouching low waiting for the shots that never materialized. Absent-mindedly Charles noticed that there was no sign of the girl. She too had hidden herself away. The next thing to strike him was that Pickle in his madness had daubed the walls with paint. WELCOME he had scrawled over and over again, as well as the slogan SAY HELLO TO FATHER JAMES.

Charles's eyes were drawn to the hideous, stinking remains of Father James. The lunatic Pickle had placed the dead priest in a chair directly beside the pulpit. Gonzales waved his hat and, disturbed by the movement, a horde of blue-black flies lifted themselves temporarily from the rotting flesh. The stench was enough to knock any normal man out, but evidently not Pickle, who had for his own unfathomable reasons holed up in this place of worship.

'Come on out, you varmint,' the renegade bellowed. 'Come on out and tell me to my face what you think of me. Let's hear your opinion, or even another sermon. I ain't particular.' He laughed. 'So you want to play hide and seek, do you! Well I am more than happy to oblige.'

There was silence except for the drone of the flies and the heavy breathing of the renegades as they moved slowly into the church. They were all on edge, ready to hit the floor at the slightest sign of trouble. It irked them that no one dared risk shooting the quarry dead. Charles wanted Pickle alive and if Charles were thwarted he was liable to fly off the handle and turn on his own with a viciousness that could not be surpassed.

Clara Russell, her heart thumping, crawled through the hole in the wall laboriously chiselled out by Will Pickle with a little help from herself. 'It's the only way to get them,' he had advised. 'There ain't no way I can take them on single-handed. These varmints should have been dealt with by the army long time back. I ain't got a death wish, Miss Clara. Fact is, I am beginning to think life is worth living again.'

She guessed, why, surely he must be smitten with Miz Jezabel, a woman Clara had been forbidden to even acknowledge.

'If you can think of a safer way to deal with them let me know,' he had said.

Reaching safety, Clara scrambled to her feet. It was up to her now. And now that it was time she found that she did not give a damn. He was right. This was the only way to deal with Crazy Charles.

The whole damn town with the exception of Miz Katy, Mrs Charlotte Cooper and Miz Gattrell, had turned against her. Sanctimously declaring that things must be done right, Walt Lock had set up an impromptu court in her own saloon. Witness after witness were eager to declare how she had turned upon Simon Parker without warning and knifed him in full view of her customers.

'He was looking for trouble,' Miz Katy yelled. 'And if Will Pickle were here you would not have put Miz Jezabel on trial. You varmints are gonna pay for this when he gets back.'

'Hell, we are doing him a favour,' Walt Lock declared. 'And if he is too crazy to see it, why, he is a dead man. Furthermore there ain't a man living who can keep me from doing my duty.'

'There ain't no need to take her out to Dora Parker's ranch,' someone yelled, a customer who hitherto had always seemed affable. 'Let's string her up in town.'

'There is every need to take her out to Dora Parker's ranch. The widow turned to me in her hour of need. Folk from town are welcome to accompany us to the hanging.' He laughed. 'Rest assured, she ain't going to escape between town and the ranch. Now let's have the verdict.'

Miz Jezabel never said a word. She did not feel a

need to justify her actions. Where the hell was Will Pickle, she thought angrily. Like all the other men she had known he had let her down.

'Are you going to watch the show?' ramrod Sid Lowe addressed Moses. 'I'll get you a chair if you like,' he volunteered generously. Word had just come from town that Miz Jezabel had been found guilty and was being escorted to the Parker ranch to get her just deserts. Lock had sent word that they must have the noose ready and waiting.

'Aah no,' the oldster wheezed. 'I think I will take a rest.'

'After it's over, after you have rested, well, I am sorry to tell you that Mrs Parker wants you off the ranch. Fact is . . .' Sid hesitated, 'Fact is she begrudges the free food you are getting. Hell, I cannot understand the woman. You're more than earning your food and she still wants you gone.'

'Is that a fact?'

'I am afraid so, old-timer.'

'Don't fret yourself, Sid. Mrs Dora Parker ain't never going to set eyes on me after today.' He cackled. 'I can vouch for that. Now you get on with your chores. Like I said, I am going to take a nap.' Moses hobbled away. Sid shook his head: old age was a terrible thing! He was relieved that he would not have to run the old varmint off the Parker spread, Moses having indicated that he would leave peacefully. And then he forgot about the old man.

If she had been expecting Will Pickle to come riding over the horizon, guns blazing, then she had been disappointed, Walt Lock thought with satisfaction as the Parker spread came into view.

The best part of the town seemed to be accompanying them. Women – and young ones too – were filling the armada of buggies and wagons that was rolling along behind the hanging-party. Why, they might have been on their way to a picnic. But that was folk for you and a hanging always brought out the worst in them, so he had observed.

Miz Jezabel had expected Moses to be amongst the assembled crowd. But there was no sign of the oldster. She then forgot about him. Lord, she had never imagined her life was destined to end this way.

The sound of the heavy doors of the church slamming shut echoed in the stillness. Men rushed the doors, only to find that they had been bolted from the outside.

'It's that damn girl. She has locked us in,' Charles yelled. He knew what was going on. 'She's making her escape. Well, it will not take long to run her down. Now spread out. Let's root him out.'

Gonzales sniffed. The stench of rotting flesh was pungent but there was something else as well, a smell that hitherto had been masked.

'Get up into the bell-tower. Blast anyone you see moving,' Charles yelled. 'Now spread out. Let's flush him out!'

Will had prudently locked the door to the bell-tower, as Charles was about to discover. He thinned his lips and prayed that all went according to plan. If not they would be upon him pretty soon. Gritting his teeth, he lit his kerosene-soaked torch, stepped out from behind a pillar and hurled the torch into the pulpit.

The base of the wooden pulpit formed a shallow bowl. Kerosene had been poured into this hollow. The pulpit ignited with a rush of flame. The kerosene that had been poured over the steps Ieading down from the pulpit also ignited. Will, on his hands and knees, crawled towards the only way out; the gap behind the altar where a slab of brick had been removed. At any moment he expected someone to blast him. But his luck held; all attention now was on the fire. He was through the gap and outside the church before they began to regain their senses.

He seemed to be filled with superhuman strength as he levered the removed slab back into place, effectively trapping the whole darn bunch of them inside the burning building. For good measure he also aimed to place a cart soaked with kerosene up against the church doors. Crazy Charles and his band of renegades were going to find there was no escape from their own little hell!

Inside the church, men screamed and cursed. The remains of poor Father James burnt fiercely now. Santino screamed: flames were licking at his legs. Some of the others were already ablaze, crashing around blindly, maddened with pain as unearthly shrieks filled the church.

'Fool!' Gonzales screamed. 'Fool!' Gonzales was ablaze. Howling, he grabbed hold of Crazy Charles, setting the renegade boss alight also. Charles screamed. Some of the men were shooting themselves. Santino howled and beat at the flames that engulfed him.

Outside Clara Russell cried as she watched the church blazing.

'We've got to be sure none of them gets out,' Will Pickle observed unnecessarily, adding: 'Well, Miss Clara, there was no other way.' He closed his ears to the piercing shrieks and the roar of the flames. 'We must put this from our minds.' He paused, 'I'll escort you to Fort Beacon.'

'Thank you kindly, Mr Pickle,' she replied. It went without saying that neither of them would reminisce about the terrible events of today. Terrible events had to be buried. It was better that way.

'Seems like more trouble heading our way,' Will declared sourly, eyeing the folk who were advancing upon them; townspeople waving sticks and some brandishing guns. A stone was thrown. Will jerked back. The missile had narrowly missed his head.

'Goddamnit!' Reacting instinctively he shot the galoot who had thrown the stone and another three for good measure. The rest of the varmints scattered.

Their horses were ready and waiting. The church roof collapsed inwards. 'Mount up, Miss Clara. We must fork it out damn quick.' He scowled. 'I guess we riled them when we torched the church. I reckon they think losing the church is more important than losing their priest!' Hell, all he could think about was getting Clara to Fort Beacon and getting himself back to Galbraith and Miz Jezabel. He had been away far too long.

*

Lieutenant Zachariah spotted the two Mexicans heading for the river. The way they spurred their horses to greater speed aroused his suspicions, Zachariah was a career officer, who had no intention of staying in this god-forsaken spot longer than he had to. He had seized the opportunity to lead a patrol in search of the renegade Crazy Charles. He had expressed outrage when the rescued women had arrived at Fort Beacon. Something had to be done and he was going to do it. Needless to say there was a reporter from an Eastern newspaper at the fort, sending back dispatches concerning frontier life.

'Head them off,' Zachariah ordered. 'If necessary shoot them out of the saddle before they get across the river.' He could see the headlines. The two became a dozen or more. The chase to head them off before they reached the river became a hard-fought battle. Unfortunately his men, following orders to the letter, blasted the two out of the saddle before they were able to reach the river.

'Riders coming, sir. A man and woman.'

Will introduced himself to the lieutenant whom he disliked on sight. Zachariah did not think much of the tall lawman, who had little to say other than that he would be obliged if Miss Clara could be escorted safely to Fort Beacon. Zachariah agreed. The way he would tell the story was that it was he who had rescued the lawman and girl.

Free of Miss Clara, Will turned his horse towards Galbraith. There was a sinking feeling in the pit of his stomach. There was no telling what Parker and Herman might have been up to in his absence. He could not trust those two varmints not to stir up trouble.

Mrs Dora Parker prolonged Miss Jezabel's discomfort by insisting that Sheriff Walt Lock take tea before they proceeded with the hanging. Miz Jezabel was forced to watch as a maid brought out a tray of tea.

'Say, Sid,' a waddy exclaimed, 'that old coot has locked himself in the stable!'

'He's probably dozed off,' Sid rejoined. 'We'll rouse him after the hanging! Let him sleep. He's running out of places to hole up.'

From the upper part of the stable Moses had a fine view of the porch and its occupants. He had decided to use his old buffalo gun. He watched Walt Lock take tea. The lawman, fool that he was, had relaxed his vigilance. Why, from the looks of it the varmint was flirting with Mrs Dora Parker.

Whistling cheerfully Moses squeezed the trigger, his shot taking Sheriff Walt Lock clean out of his chair. Blood spread over the man's shirt. Lock died instantly. The second bullet struck Deputy Jackson and the third killed Mrs Dora Parker. Chaos had broken out amongst the watchers. Moses was pleased to see that Hughie, the stage driver, possessed sufficient wits to cut Miz Jezabel free. To ensure that attention did not focus upon the two Moses turned his gun on fleeing townsfolk. He shot indiscriminately and found that he was enjoying himself.

Grabbing Miz Jezabel's arm, Hughie steered her towards a horse. 'Ain't no need to fret, Miz Jezabel,' he reassured her. 'Why, I reckon it must be old Moses having himself a party. There ain't no way he is going to blast us by mistake. Yessir, that old varmint still has his wits about him.'

He shoved her on to a horse. Miz Jezabel was in shock. Men and women were falling like sitting ducks.

'Why?' she croaked.

Hughie steered them away from the Parker spread. 'Well, old Moses owed Will Pickle a favour, seeing as how Will overlooked his one lapse. Yep, Moses always reckoned Will was sweet on you, Miz Jezabel.'

'They're falling like flies!'

'Well, that's the way of it, Miz Jezabel. He ain't got nothing to lose. He's blasted a lawman and shot womenfolk. They'll string him up for sure if they get him. But I don't reckon they will. Old Moses is coming to the end of his journey and he is going out with a bang.'

She felt as though she did not know Hughie at all, this man who drove the stage and seemed unperturbed by the massacre taking place in their wake.

'There's only one way to look at things, Miz Jezabel. This ain't our concern. It's not any of our doing. And there was nothing we could have done to prevent it.'

'But you knew.'

'I sure as hell didn't. Old Moses never confided in me,' Hughie retorted indignantly. 'Now let's get the hell out of here, Miz Jezabel. You ain't out of hot water yet.'

Moses had run out of shells. He could hear them

down below breaking down the door of the stable. The horses were going wild. It all seemed far, far away and there was a terrible pain in his chest. He settled back against the straw, 'That showed 'em,' he muttered.

Ramrod Sid Lowe was first through the door. He expected to be blasted. Nothing happened. Plucking up courage Sid put a ladder in place and clambered up to the upper reaches of the stable. The old man lay there, quite dead, quite unlike the Moses they had known. He gazed upwards, the light gone from his eyes.

'Well,' Sid pronounced, 'I blame Sheriff Walt Lock for all of this. He ought to have had more sense. And no,' he rounded on a waddy who had spoken up, '*no*! We ain't going to look for Miz Jezabel. That woman is poison and Will Pickle is welcome to her. That's all I've got to say on the matter.'

Will Pickle, getting a fresh horse, left Galbraith at the gallop. All he could think about was Miz Jezabel hanging at the end of a rope. And it was his goddamn fault. He ought to have been there to look out for her. He had let her down. He'd hunt down Walt Lock. He'd kill Mrs Dora Parker himself. Why, he'd burn Galbraith to the ground. He'd be a broken man for the rest of his life if he lost Miz Jezabel. And he damn well knew his late wife would have heartily approved of the way Miz Jezabel had dealt with Simon Parker. Gertrude Pickle herself had possessed a fearsome temper when roused.

He found Miz Jezabel and Hughie on the trail leading to town. They both spoke at once, Miz

Jezabel demanding to know what had taken him so long and Hughie explaining that Moses had saved the day. Leastways, he had saved Miz Jezabel.

'All those dead folk,' Miz Jezabel muttered.

Will took a deep breath. Dead folk did not concern him. 'I am through with Galbraith, Miz Jezabel, and I reckon you are too. I have only two things to say.' He paused.

'Get on with it!'

'I'd be honoured if you would do me the honour of becoming Mrs Pickle. And, we've got to go somewhere, Miz Jezabel, where trouble won't find us. How do you feel about shipping out? A long sea-voyage ought to keep us out of trouble. What do you say?'

'Maybe,' she agreed, not wanting to appear too eager.

'Just get the hell out of it, the pair of you,' Hughie advised. 'I'm heading into Galbraith to get Miz Gatrell. There's no telling how many Moses has blasted.'

'Well, we ain't staying around to find out,' Will rejoined.

Hughie watched them ride away. He reckoned they'd make it.